To Dear

Life Passing By

You're Never Too Old to Come Out

Hope you get a chance to read it. :)

By Matthew Campling

Matthew

May 2023

Life passing by

This book was first published in Great Britain in paperback during August 2021.

ISBN: 978-1916180383

About the Author:

Matthew's career has been shared between being a psychotherapist (MA Psychotherapy, BA Hons Counselling) and many writing jobs. He's been a magazine Features Editor and Assistant Editor and a columnist for film and theatre. For 10 years he wrote advice columns as an agony uncle, and he was a regular guest expert on TV and radio, especially on ITV's 'Trisha' show. He is a multi-award nominated playwright and has had 11 stage plays performed. He lives in North London.

Other Books by this Author

Fiction

The Secondary Victim
Who Is Killing All My Ex-Boyfriends?
Invitation to a Haunting
The Dead House

Non-Fiction

Eating Disorder Self-Cure
Therapeutic Weight Loss
The 12-Type Enneagram
Diary of a Male Anorexic

Dedication

For Harry

Acknowledgments

Thanks to Dr Steve Green for his professional help, designing the cover and preparing the book for publication.

Early readers of the book: Susan Milford, Harry Hicks, Gerry McGee.

One. ALEC

It could be a delightful setting. Gothic influence, marvelous old brick. Past the carpark there's an arch with neatly trimmed lawns and shrubs beyond. Sad that no one's here for the building, only for the ceremonies it hosts. The other day I read that Matt Monro, the famous former bus driver, the singer of *Born Free* and *From Russia With Love*, was cremated here, in Golders Green cemetery. Little man, you know. He was five foot six inches tall and used to tell his audiences that he was not only a singer, he was a mind reader. For example he could tell what they were all thinking: 'Isn't he short?' This makes me smile and I catch the eye of Alison's sister, Rebecca, who's come up from Taunton in Devon for the funeral. Her eyes are red and she pushes past a couple of neighbours to stand next to me. She reaches for my hand and I oblige.

'Alec, such a terrible day' she says. I look up at the clear blue sky, the softly golden sun.

'Yes we've been lucky. With the weather' I answer. She is about to argue, to perhaps rebuke me for my insensitivity. Then she remembers that I'm chief mourner, the widower, Ground Zero of the bereaved. She realises that I don't know what I'm saying. Instead she squeezes my hand then lets go as she sees Robert, mutual cousin of hers and my late wife and the most successful member of our family. She's away, her broad beam weaving through the throng like a well-fed shark combining mourning with sucking up to riches.

I'm getting a handle on what it means to be the widower. Basically I can say and do exactly what I like and it all gets put down to the bereavement. I think some of that's true, and I do keep having to remind myself that Alison is actually dead. I suppose I am in shock although these feelings aren't like the emotions I experienced when our son died. That was sheer blinding gut-churning misery but this, so far at least, has its positive points. No one who really knew us would assume I would be grief-stricken by her death. She was a good woman, she was loyal and kind. She was thoughtful. She never said anything worth listening to and we both knew we were in a poor marriage.

This thought causes me to frown and Dennis, one of the other partners in my family's business, appears by my side. 'It gets easier 'he says as though I asked his opinion which I never do. 'We're lucky with the weather today' I respond. The same tender expression appears in his eyes as Alison's, that 'The old boy is unhinged and we can't blame him' gleam.

'Do you want some help carrying the coffin? 'he asks. I look at him.

'I believe we have professionals to do that' I reply. I indicate a clump of four or five men, identically dressed in morning coats and striped trousers. My original vision also included top hats but apparently they can fall off, leading to an unfortunate hat-chasing when we require slow and dignified progress. On the other hand, I think hat-chasing might give this event the touch of humour it desperately needs.

'Yes of course' says Dennis. 'Sorry I don't know what I'm thinking. Alison's death was such a terrible shock. You must have been so shocked.'

I've already used up my line about the weather so I merely murmur 'I'm devastated.' Dennis goes off happily to spread the news that I'm devastated and as he reaches each little group they all turn to me with almost identical expressions of sorrow. I am not used to so much attention so I look around for a distraction. I wonder if all the pallbearers are dressed exactly the same? The trousers look identical, and the coats. I imagine the scene backstage, the group squeezing into hired attire, fumbling for their turn in front of the mirror. I wonder if they have showers beforehand? Communal showers? I become aware of one of the pallbearers specifically. His is not the broadest back or the tallest height. Yet he stands out, partly because of his air of innocence, as though he has wandered in from the fields where he was tending a flock of lambs, and partly because his profile would be of interest to Raphael. His eyes from where I am standing look green and his hair is auburn. It's a little long which emphasises his fragility.

Usually I would be too guarded to tease out these physical specificities yet now who is there to stop me? Who is there at home to make me feel bad because I've watched a football match and been more interested in the footballers' thighs than the ball work? I've attended matches because it got me away from Alison on a Saturday afternoon, and because every now and then I saw a young man to whom I could attach a private fantasy. Now I don't have to worry anymore because Alison is safely laid to rest and I no longer have to pretend.

At this thought, of not having to pretend any longer, and also still observing the beautiful shepherd/pallbearer's softly chiseled profile, my eyes fill with tears. Automatically I reach for my hankie and gently touch the sides. This signal brings Helen, one of Alison's closest friends, to comfort me.

'She loved you so much 'she howls, wiping her own face with a ridiculously crumpled and damp tissue. I consider using the weather line on her then tire of its limitations, so I pat her on the back. This surprises her and her hat tilts louchely to one side. I hope no one will tell her because she looks a perfect scream. She looks like she's been at the races and had one too many after her outside fancy came first at 40 to 1. I can feel a bubble of laughter pushing its way up inside me and turn this into a cough. Helen immediately looks extremely anxious.

'Alec, have you caught a cold?'

'I don't think so. We've been so lucky with the weather.'

'You do know you can rely on Bobby and I? This is our open invitation to lean on us as much as you like. Would you like me to organise dinner this evening?'

Helen, in my experience, is a genuinely kind person. I used to watch her and my wife circulating at parties, a few kind words to this person, a thoughtful suggestion to that. Charming behaviour. I speak with genuine warmth.

'No thank you, dear. I'm making arrangements.'

Her compassionate eyes fill with tears. 'Don't think you have to be brave.'

I smile in reply. 'I never think of myself as brave. I've always been one of nature's designated cowards.'

Her responding smile is wreathed with tender pity. She thinks I'm joking but being a coward has always been my downfall. She moves away, her eyes on compassionate full beam, searchlighting the crowd for indications of significant grief. The last thing I feel like today is having dinner with Helen and Bobby. I always think they would be happier visiting leper colonies where their overt need to care for others would achieve full actualisation. They're too good for local charity work, they deserve a full-blown pandemic.

One of the pallbearers, unfortunately not the shepherd, approaches me. He speaks softly, obsequiously, which annoys me because I'm not glass and I don't need to be mollycoddled.

'Sir, if everyone's here we should make a start. It's a long service.'

Yes, and that's not my doing. Alison wasn't one for a fancy service. Being, as I've already noted, spineless, I bowed to pressure from various friends of hers who want to say something personal. At one point there were so many I was beginning to think there wouldn't be anyone in the stalls to hear except me. And the last thing I need, especially today, is to reminded of what I have lost. Of the woman I lived with for over thirty years. Of the family we raised, the son we lost.

The service isn't that bad. There was a dramatic moment when the hearse arrived out of nowhere, drawn by two magnificent black horses with fuming black feather plumes. The pallbearers efficiently shouldered the polished mahogany coffin and carried it into the chapel. There was a sufficient crowd to fill all the pews and there was even a modest standing room only attendance. All of this is testament to the goodness of my late wife. I was pleased that her passing has been marked by a respectful and genuine coming together of people who cared about her.

My own feelings, of course, are more complicated. I know that in the months to come I will have a plethora of time to comb out the tangled emotions I have felt and continue to feel about my late wife. Perhaps the young shepherd would like to drop round for a drink and listen while I dredge up anecdote after anecdote of our more than three decades together? After the service concludes, when the coffin disappears behind the curtains which then close, and any of the mourners who've been saving the best till last finally let go with loud sobbings, I look around for my shepherd but he has already left. For a moment an image of him naked, in the shower, one of the other pallbearers handing him the soap, pops unbidden and lustfully into my imagination. Yet I then turn away from this image, mindful that after all this is my opportunity to bid an honest goodbye to Alison, and that I do not want to confuse my genuine feelings of sadness with any private feeling.

Nearly everyone comes back to our house for an informal wake. Helen has coordinated a heaving dining table of assorted foodstuffs. You would think the mourners had been at the crematorium for a fortnight rather than fifty minutes from the enthusiastic way the refreshments are greeted. Glints of white side plates and flashing silver forks, fluttering damask napkins and excited chatter. Helen appears beside me, her face set in grim satisfaction.

'I thought I'd over catered but I think we'll do fine.'

'Thank you, Helen. You've been a marvel.'

She grasps my hand and stares compassionately into my watery brown eyes.

'Anything at all. You know that. We're there for you.'

I nod and shake my hand free. If I wanted to, I could stand on the table and drop my trousers. This is my day too, and any outrages of behaviour from me today would be put down to a temporary unhinging of my right mind. I spot the teenage sons of one of our other neighbours. They have crammed their plates full of treats and are bolting them down, presumably so they can return for seconds.

'Hello boys 'I greet them cheerily. The one continues eating but the other stops long enough to give me a nod.

'Hello Mr Bland. Sorry about your loss.'

'Oh that's all right 'I say. 'And do call me Alec. Any time you want to use the pool, just send me a text and then jump in.'

The two teenagers exchange a look. The subject of our private pool has long been a source of discontent and resentment among the locals. Where we live, Hampstead Garden Suburb, is a haven of green hedges, neat lawns, no shops and definitely no pubs. When Dame Henrietta Barnett, the brains behind our garden suburb, put her community-based plans into effect she wanted nothing to disturb the perfect English sense of Arts and Craft houses, well-tended flower beds, and no commercial activities of any sort.

It was Alison, wielding her ongoing back problem like a mace, who managed to bully the usually implacable Community Trust into allowing us to build what we billed as a ‘hydro-therapeutic pool.’ Of course we’ve used it as a general pool and if we have children round the happy screams can be heard up and down the block. It’s always irritated me and the noise has cut into my pleasant, quiet afternoons of reading in my study. Now that Alison has moved on it had suddenly occurred to me that the pool, expensively maintained and kept at a delightful 82 degrees, could become a gathering point for the more interesting of our neighbours.

‘Yeah, that sounds great’ says the older, Ned. His brother, still eating, looks surprised and looks to Ned for further clarification.

‘Yeah, we could bring a whole gang of us around, thanks ’he says. My mind instantly fills with horror. The last thing I’m looking for is a pool full of rowdy teenagers and their charmless girlfriends.

‘Perhaps give me time to adjust to widowerhood ’I say hastily and move away. I resolve to have the pool emptied as soon as possible in case they don’t drop the idea. I look around for someone I actually want to talk to and see only Dennis. I wave to beckon him and he moves his way round two women I have never seen before who are eating and talking simultaneously.

‘Alec, old cock ’he says.

‘I know, don’t remind me ’I respond with a slightly roguish smile. Dennis looks confused.

‘Good job the weather held’ I continue. His face clears.

‘Yes. Terrific. I mean, dreadfully sad about Alison. Good weather, though. I can picture her in heaven, arriving on a good day.’

Honestly what people say when they feel obliged to offer a few words.

'That's why I had her wearing her red dress, you know 'I say. He looks confused. 'Yes, you see Alison was always so colourless. Well not so much colourless, as beige. Always blending into the background. I thought if she turned up at the pearly gates in a red dress, she'd catch the eye of Archangel Michael and possibly get a jump on the crowd.'

I can clearly see on Dennis's face the thought that the old boy's mind has definitely unhinged with grief and that he'd better humour me.

'Yes, that was forward thinking.'

'Don't want poor Alison shoved to the back because of her beige dress and brown handbag. If I'd thought about it, I'd have bought her one of those glittery Chanel bags to make absolutely sure she'll stand out.'

Dennis is resolved to be compassionate. 'Alec, if there's anything we can do for you…'

This sparks an interesting realisation: I don't, really, know what I want or like. I've spent my whole life trying to be what first my father and then my wife demanded I be so I can't decide for myself now. I speak my mind.

'I have no idea what I want, Dennis. My mind is a complete fog.'

'Of course, old man 'he says.

'Can you not keep calling me old 'I snap. 'I'm seventy-one. I'm not dead yet.'

He burbles hastily 'Of course not. Sorry I don't know why I've suddenly started using those words. None of us think of you as old.'

This is a lie. I know when people hear I'm seventy-one they look surprised. I used to think it was because I look younger until I put the various comments together and worked out it was because they had assumed I'm older. It's true that I've never taken off a pound so whatever I put on stays with me forever. It's also true that the many hours I've spent on the family business, tracking long columns and determining exactly what has happened to every penny that's come into the family accounts has left me looking like an exhausted walrus. A walrus. Not my conception, something I overheard one of the middle managers calling me at last year's Christmas party. The full comment was 'He's a loveable old walrus' so it could have been worse but it's still not a *soubriquet* I am happy to own.

'I'm just looking forward to some peace and quiet while I work out what I'm going to do for the rest of my life 'I explain.

'Yes, and you might want to go away for a nice, restful holiday 'he responds.

'I thought I might go to Las Vegas' I respond. 'And spend some of the family money on Cristal champagne and prostitutes.'

The crowd in our dining room has up till this moment been fulsome and the only way one can communicate is to raise one's voice above the heaving throng. Of course at this moment there is one of those sudden, unpredicted silences so my future plans ring around the room. There is a pause and then Helen saves the day.

'Oh what a lovely notion' she cries.

'Yes' says Bobby, catching her meaning, 'why don't we all go to Las Vegas!'

They are dear people. My ridiculous comment is quickly forgotten in an excited babble about the pros and cons of behaving recklessly. Within an hour the last straggler, clutching as much food as I can prevail upon them to carry away, has departed. I sit, nursing a Lemsip just in case I do have a cold, and ruminate on how the day has gone.

'It's a good job I didn't say everything I was thinking 'I say out loud. There is a shuffling noise and one of the neighbour's sons comes out from behind the piano.

'Sorry Mr. Bland, what was that?'

'Oh Paul! Thought you'd gone. Take something from the drinks table on your way out.'

Paul grunts with pleasure, selects a nearly full bottle of Scotch and bounces out cheerily. It's a damn good job I didn't say everything I was thinking. Because if I had shared with the group that my reason for going to Las Vegas was to buy Cristal champagne and *male* prostitutes, then rather than amused indulgence no doubt I would have been pilloried. And after all, I observe as I move my tongue round the bottom of the cup, tasting the bitter dregs of the cold remedy, I don't even know if that's what I want to do. For all I know I'm completely asexual. Or I do actually fancy women and it was just Alison I never, ever fancied. Perhaps when I look at a young man and my heart jumps, perhaps what I'm really doing is connecting with my lost youth. Youth that was never mine even back in the day. All I know is that I'm now seventy-one and if there was a walrus line-up they'd ask me to join in. I'm alone for the first time in my life and I would like this aloneness to mean something. I could just continue to go along the downward path like Alison, letting go life piece by piece until there's only a shriveled up and drained husk of life, a joyless shell, spending 18 hours a day asleep and in the six awake, dreaming of the grave and silence. It's a terrible feeling, to acknowledge that life is passing one by.

Or I could take myself in hand and try to reverse the long and bitter years of deprivation, denial and abstinence. I don't know what the market may be like for someone with my C.V. I'm not naïve enough to believe someone would want me for myself, but I have a lovely house and plenty of money in the bank and I can probably put together a portfolio of attractive points that surely someone will be interested in? At least I no longer have to keep lying in order to respect my father or honour my wife. I will visit my son's grave and leave flowers in

Alison's name. But then through all the rest of my days I've only got myself to think about. What a lovely thought.

Two. GUY

I stay in bed and watch my lover as he strides round our bedroom nude, carefully assembling his outfit for the day. When we first met his morning routine was different. He would throw himself out of bed in a tousled wreck and grab the stained T-shirt and pants he'd dumped in a heap the previous night. Now he takes a couturier's pride in donning an immaculate ensemble, yet does he know that I used to love him in his dirty T?

He stands for a moment, enjoying the rays of the morning sun on his taut, elongated torso. He flexes and in response, under the duvet, my cock rouses itself with potential business. I know that I need only flick back the cover and Ted will drop his socks, return to our bed and with his arms supporting his body like a lizard… No, stop. Instead I push myself harder into the pillow and ponder for the twentieth time why I no longer desire the man I live with. Of course I know. When we met, he was a street urchin. Looking into his troubled, needy eyes filled my heart with previously untapped depths of tenderness. I recall his joyful relief when I invited him to move in and his simple excitement when he began studying to be an insurance rep. Now I watch through weary eyelids as he drapes his body with his work disguise. There was a time I would wake in the night, see him sleeping gently next to me, and my need to possess him was so intense and greedy I'd have to wake him and have him before we both fell into exhausted and fulfilled rest. Now all I crave is that he goes out and stays away until my evening drinks have mellowed me to the point at which I can tolerate his inevitable monologue about his less than fascinating day peddling life insurance to perfectly healthy people.

It's not his fault. At the beginning I was charmed to hear his progress. It's just that when he no longer turned to me for advice and support, I lost the connection I thought we had. I am so bored that I know it will not be forever before I break through my carapace of stoicism and tell him to leave. It won't be that simple since we bought this place with a combined mortgage. At the moment I lack the financial resources to buy out his half. Also there isn't anyone else I'm interested in so it's not as though he's getting in the way. Actually he retains vestiges of his former sweetness. Now, as he readies to leave, there's a poignancy in his approaching our bed, bending over to plant a moist kiss on my lips.

I'll be back by eight he says.

That's fine my last client leaves at seven fifty-five I reply.

He queries I thought you had an early client?

I grunt. When I got up in the night to use the toilet, he'd left me a message cancelling this morning.

Sorry about that.

Don't be. He's within my strict forty-eight-hour notice period so he has to pay.

That's good. Go back to sleep. I love you heaps.

Have a profitable day I reply.

He hesitates then he walks out. He knows something has changed yet being an introvert he won't ask me. He doesn't want it spelled out.

I take a shower. As the hot water runs fluid fingers into my muscles and cracks, I remember how he was when we first met. Instantly my groin beast inflates to its full length and I squirt a dab of soap on myself and wake myself up properly.

Afterwards I pad barefoot over to the weights stacked neatly in the corner. At 51 I can't rely on nature to do the work anymore. I need three heavy workouts a week or my body begins to lose its definition. I know it upsets Ted that I keep my body trim while he no longer has the same rights over it. At least he's stopped trying to trick me into sex. Now when we turn out the light it's only a companionable, moist kiss then we turn our backs on each other.

My second appointment this morning is a newby. After breakfast I run around, turning a corner of the combined open plan sitting/dining/kitchen into my therapeutic space. From the notes I took over the phone when he answered my ongoing ad in Therapy Central, I know he's 71 and recently suffered a bereavement. He gave his address as Hampstead so I'm hoping he's in sufficient funds to be a nice, regular, weekly client. I really need to boost my incomings if I'm going to buy Ted out.

He's on time which is a good sign. I open the door and smile. He looks like a walrus, a particularly sad and nervous example of the species. I increase my smile and top it up with a sympathetic tilt of the head. He follows me into my space and drinks greedily from the waiting water glass. We face each other and I wait for him to begin.

'Thanks for seeing me at such short notice.'

'I have more availability in the day.'

'Oh yes of course. I suppose people have to go to work to make the money to pay you. I work, but I am in charge.'

'Did your husband die suddenly? 'I ask and he looks confused.

'My wife 'he replies and I mutter an apology. It's clear on my site I'm a gay man and my clients, principally, are gay men so I wait for him to explain.

'My wife of over thirty years. We married because my father told me I was nearly forty and it was a disgrace I wasn't married. I was happy living my celibate life. Not hurting anyone. He introduced me to my wife and we got married and I think I hurt her.'

‘Can I ask you a personal question? Did you know you were gay?’

He stares at me mournfully.

‘I don’t know what I am, Guy. Is it all right if I call you Guy?’

‘Please. I’ll call you Alec.’

‘Oh yes please do. My wife’s just died of cancer. Stomach cancer. I suppose all those years she was angry with me, kept it inside, pretended everything was all right. She liked being my wife, of course, she enjoyed many financial and material benefits…’

He stares into space and I shift in my seat. It’s very easy to feel empathy for this man’s situation. ‘Is that what you want to talk about?’

‘Oh, one of the things, my guilt about marrying my wife when I was never attracted. In the beginning she was lively, and most people thought her pretty. She soon learned I was not emotionally demonstrative. The only times I ever saw her angry was over the question of a child, of children. I didn’t want them, partly because I didn’t know if I could stay erect that long. I don’t know how I did it, I suppose I have just enough in me to stay erect when there’s no other way. We had a son.’

I turn my supportive smile into a happy one. It’s what’s expected when children are mentioned.

‘My son, Cecil, he died. Oh, there were problems at birth and he didn’t live with us, he lived in a Home. He died when he was 14. Strange sort of God that causes a boy to be born and then deprives him of life. Sorry, are you religious?’

‘I’m not ’I reply, ‘and even if I were you’d still be free to say exactly what you like in here.’

‘Oh. Right. Yes. I have no idea what I want to say.’

'But … you do think you're gay?'

'Oh absolutely. I've never fancied women. I've had endless platonic one-sided passions for unsuitable men. When I was younger I wasn't like I am now. I did have a few opportunities. People you wouldn't suspect. Friends of the family. Men who were also fathers. It's so complicated. Of course now it's marvelous, men can get married. I wonder what my father would have said if I'd agreed to get married but introduced a boy rather than a girl. He'd probably not have laughed. He didn't have a sense of humour or anything else usually attributable to a human being.

'My great-great-great grandfather was an ambitious servant who made violent advances to the eldest, unmarried, daughter of the house. It was thought almost a miracle that my great-great grandfather was born, although it has also been rumoured that a maid and the family's second son may have supplied the semen and the womb. By the time my father was born there were two generations of gentility. My father was a bully and a brute. Once when I was little and singing a popular song he deliberately shut my fingers in a door to keep me quiet. See how my little finger faces outward?

'There was never any doubt that I would go to his public school, that I would marry, that I would one day be Chairman of the board. I was the only one with doubt and I must again stress how much in terror I always was of my father.'

I smile empathetically. 'I'm beginning to understand. You've had to be someone else and now your wife is dead you want to be yourself.'

He stares at me with startled eyes. 'How did you know that?'

'Because you told me. I'm only summarising.'

'Well. Yes. So I thought some therapy would help.'

'Can I ask you: have you *ever* had sex with a man?'

'Apart from some guilty wanking at public school? No. Sometimes I thought I would die from physical isolation but there was always the office, the board, Alison did a lot of entertaining. And Cecil, for a time. Life goes on, years go by and suddenly I'm a widower and seventy-one. At work I was referred to recently as a loveable old walrus.'

I flinch and begin to hastily deny this when I remember he's come here to confront the truth so instead I nod in agreement.

'So how do you think coming here can help? 'I ask.

'Can I ask you a personal question? Do you have a boyfriend?'

I let a beat go by before answering. Some therapists turn the question back, asking why the client wants to know, but I prefer to be straightforward.

'Yes. I share with my partner.'

'Do you have a photo of the two of you?'

Again I let a beat pass between us. 'Yes but I'm not comfortable with sharing it with you. Perhaps when we know each other better.'

He nods amiably at this. I'm remembering another elderly client I had a couple of years back. At that time I had been so proud of my handsome young boyfriend and I shared a photo with the other client of Ted and I on the beach. Unfortunately the other client's interest didn't stop there. Rather than talk about himself in session he wanted more and more detail of our lives together. I got that in one way we were being a model for him, but then he wanted to know sexual details. Finally I had to ask him to stop coming. So I don't want to encourage the same unhelpful development here.

We discuss how often Alec would like to attend sessions. We agree to two sessions a week and since he doesn't mention discounts I don't either. Everything about Alec indicates a considerable degree of wealth and that makes a pleasant surprise. Although I'm in Zone Two it's the scrag end of Archway and most of my clients have to balance their budgets carefully. Five minutes before time is up Alec calls for an Uber and he departs exactly on time. It seems to give him satisfaction, having some control over his day. After he leaves I make some brief notes, clear the glasses and prepare for my next client. I fall into an amusing reverie where I suggest to Alec that he takes Ted off my hands. In reality that's not an option. Ted still prefers an older man but he's not a grandad fucker. No, my domestic difficulties will need to be sorted out by me. When the time comes.

Three. ALEC

Eight days after the cremation and already people are going on with their lives. The first morning I felt besieged by contacts with the outside world. Once they had made their obligatory call to ensure I was still alive my phone hasn't bleeped in forty-eight hours. Helen and Bobby, of course, are the exception, they had me over for dinner last night. Today I've been sorting out some of Alison's clothes. When my mother died my father paid people to immediately strip the family house of every shred of her presence. He never forgave her for putting herself beyond his rage and petty revenge.

Now that I've finished as much as I can do today, I'm looking out the window. Ours is one of Hampstead Garden Suburb's minority of fully detached houses. In The Suburb, as it's always referred to, there are principally terrace rows and semi-detached residences. Even Henrietta Barnett's house is semi-detached, part of her deliberate wish for people to live in community. There were some detached residences built, though, and ours is free of extraneous noise coming through the otherwise party wall. It's very quiet, too quiet for me to bear it much longer.

So now I'm speeding towards London's Soho in the back of an Uber. I researched Gay Bars and have a list with some promising suggestions.

Now I'm standing in Old Compton Street which I've hitherto been aware has a high percentage of gay people although Alison and I have never so much as ventured along it. I would have liked to, you know, just to see what was here but Alison had a sixth sense about anything even remotely gay. We didn't even watch films like *La Cage Au Folles* or *Priscilla, Queen of the Desert.* Without her saying, it was as though she instinctively didn't want me to be reminded of anything beyond respectability and heterosexuality. I wonder if there was a conversation we should have had? With a sigh I reflect that that conversation will never happen now.

I'm standing in front of a bar called Compton's. I've had a look at another couple of likely venues, however they seemed to cater only for men under 30 and I've no desire to stand out. I've been here long enough to see men over fifty entering so this looks hopeful.

Inside it's fairly well attended. No one's smoking of course so it looks like less of a house of ill repute and more like a group of bored men nursing drinks. I buy a drink and attempt to engage the barman in small talk. I once read in a copy of Gay Times that someone left on the bus that by doing that I can indicate to the other men that I am not standoffish. He talks to me for a minute then is called away so I sip my drink and look around. Whenever I've read about gay men getting together socially the heterosexual writer notes that the air is thick with aftershave. I'm sniffing and not smelling anything. Must be a misconception or perhaps the writer is being paid by purveyors of smellies to bump up their sales. In fact the only person in the place wearing aftershave is me and it will be the last time.

I get jostled by customers at the bar, so I take up a position leaning on one of the walls. When I've been here a minute I realise I've chosen well because I'm right next to the toilet door and anyone visiting the facilities has to go right past me. I smile benignly at the customers until one man about 35 gives me a huge glare and I realise it could look like I'm trying to pick men up. This so intimidates me that I quit my advantageous perch and find a convenient corner in which to hide. Going by the number of heads now turned in the same direction there appears to be something of distinct interest coming through the main doors. By shifting sideways and tilting my head to an unnatural angle I see that a group of five men, similarly dressed in tight tops and trousers, have entered and are preening and chatting while one of their members organises drinks. With a thrill of surprise I realise one of them is the shepherd from my late wife's cremation! Small world!

I wait until he has a drink, then I reflect that I could have offered to buy him one. No matter, I still push my way over to them and give him a friendly wave and a smile. He looks at me for one split second then turns his back on me. He doesn't understand. I move round to face him and wave. 'Hello! It's Alec Bland. You buried my wife eight days ago.'

I'm shouting loud enough to be heard over the din. I realise the five men comprise the four pallbearers and a guest. The shepherd scowls.

'I'm drinking with my mates. Piss off.' I can feel my smile falling and look around desperately for inspiration. 'This is the first time I've been in a gay bar 'I shout.

Up close I see his face is not so cherubic. He leans forward to shout. 'So? Fancy your chances? The only way old blokes like you get sex is if you pay for it.'

Then he and his friends push their way past the crowd and move up the stairs to the balcony above. I'm left feeling breathless, humiliated, exposed. I fumble my way to the toilet, almost overwhelmed by the smell of urine and cheap antiseptic wash, and blunder into one of the narrow stalls. Here I slam the door and sit on the toilet seat. The pungent smell continues to assail my nostrils and my nose starts to weep. I pull toilet roll from the metal holder and realise my eyes are also weeping. I do my best to clean up both and stare at the black painted door. On it some phone numbers have been scratched with sharp objects. I have my mobile, I could call some of them. Yet I am now certain that if I did all I would get is more humiliation. Instead I sit on the seat until someone bangs on the door and I acknowledge that I'm blocking traffic. I make my apologetic way past a little queue of irritated drinkers and find myself back on the street. On my way out someone thrusts something into my hand and once I've gathered my bearings I lean against a wall and flick through a free magazine. It seems to cover the week in male strippers and transvestite acts, which is interesting. Of greater interest are some pages at the back where various services are offered.

I've never considered having to pay for sex. I've never been tempted. However I do feel tender right now, and looking through the advertisements I see a photo for a young man who seems both attractive and sympathetic. Also available immediately.

It's twenty minutes later and I'm standing outside his door. From inside I can hear what sounds like a domestic argument. Perhaps I took down the details wrongly? Nevertheless I ring the bell, which doesn't work. I bang on the door which bruises my knuckles. The door is thrown open by a tall man with painted nails.

'Uh hello. Is Jerry available?'

The man rolls his eyes, cups his one hand into a funnel and bellows 'Jessica, one for you!' He then stomps off and after a moment a man appears who I first think must be mistaken identity but when he smiles I see enough similarity between him and the photo to conclude this is the man but fifteen years later and considerably heavier.

'I can come back if it's not a good time 'I say hopefully. Jerry sighs deeply as though he's about to do what he most loathes in the world. Then he beckons me in with a desultory gesture and moves into the murk of the flat itself. I find myself in a dirty room with a double bed. Jerry hastily attempts to tidy the bed and the floor.

'Take your clothes off. Have you come far?'

I pause. For the first time in my life I am about to take off my clothes with another man in the room and in a sexual context. I cannot move. I stare at him until I vaguely remember the question he has asked.

‘Uh, yes, from Hampstead ’I reply.

He smirks. ‘Lots of very sexy houses in Hampstead I should be charging you double. What?!’ The last is not to me, it’s to the other occupant of the flat, who has appeared imperiously in the doorway.

‘I bet you haven’t washed the cover today. What have I told you?’

‘Fuck off ’says Jerry. Then he turns to me and his expression changes into a hideous caricature of desirability. ‘You and me is going to have a sexy time’ he threatens.

I’m ready to pay anything just to get out of this terrible situation but then he removes his shirt and I see he’s still got some pectoral definition. And he doesn’t appear to be put off by my appearance. So I remove my clothes, keeping my underpants on, and lie down as he indicates on the bed.

There’s a sudden bang on the now closed door. ‘I’m ordering Indian’ cries the flat’s other occupant.

‘I’ll have my usual’ shouts Jerry.

‘Perhaps we can do this some other time’ I mutter into a pillow which reeks of hair oil. In reply Jerry leans over me and flicks on the radio. Perhaps the intention is mood music but what emerges are two channels, one superimposed on the other, one of rap music and the other some foreign person shouting. I have never heard such a babble yet Jerry seems satisfied. He picks up a bottle of baby oil from the floor and pours too much of it on his hands. He leans over me and begins to knead my shoulders and the top of my back. Up till now I’ve been clinging onto the hope that Jerry has actually trained in physical massage but as his fingers twist and pummel my flesh I give up that hope and concentrate on not shouting with pain.

After a few minutes he removes his trousers and he’s not wearing underwear. His private parts are unusually large and that could have been appealing but the smell accompanying this action seems to indicate that Jerry takes a bath like our dear Queen Victoria: once a month whether she needs it or not. Jerry needs it.

He brings his genitals closer to me and I have to turn the other way. He then transfers his attentions to my own private parts. You might have thought that a professional offering 'happy endings' as per his advert might possess even the most rudimentary idea of how to give pleasure to another man. No, Jerry seems to have learned his physical skills laying bricks and mortar. After a minute I pull myself up.

'You done then? 'he asks with genuine hope.

'Definitely 'I say.

Jerry wipes his greasy hands on the bedcover.

'Ok that's a hundred and twenty quid you owe me 'he reports.

I stare indignantly. 'It's not the money' I say. 'I was promised an intimate shower for two afterwards.'

'Yeah,' notes Jerry, 'shower's bust.'

'How am I supposed to put my clothes back on? 'I ask. 'I'm covered with baby oil.'

'Yeah' nods Jerry in agreement.

'I have to have a shower!' I snap. Jerry shrugs and at that moment his flat mate enters.

'I've fixed the shower curtain' he announces. Jerry smirks. 'Great. Come this way please.'

I waddle past them, clutching my underpants to my genitals. The bathroom is tiny and although it was originally white it is now every sordid shade of sick yellow, off beige and grimy brown. The shower is in the bath. The bath has a shower curtain. I am not good with climbing into baths but with the two of them watching I carefully step into the bath. It is equipped with one of those mini water heaters they fob you off with on foreign holidays which I have always found singularly inadequate. Especially for removing a great deal of baby oil from my body. However I work out how to obtain the trickle of water it supplies, smile at the two men, pull the shower curtain and the clumsily-erected edifice collapses, banging my head as it goes.

I clean myself up as well as I can using toilet roll and the sink. As I move back to the bedroom I hear Jerry saying that in a couple of weeks he's moving to an exclusive Mayfair apartment and I must remember to take his card.

I count out the money carefully into his hand. As he is checking it, I cannot stop myself saying 'I hope you get more enjoyment out of spending it than I've had.' He looks at me and smiles ingenuously. 'Thanks. I'm going to Gran Canaria next week matter of fact. Want to come with?' I'm about to think of something really remarkably rude in reply when he adds 'My daily rate is three hundred quid and of course you'll have to pay for the room and the flight and the food. I can buy my own drinks.'

I feel so assailed by how very, very different my life has been compared to this man's that I am stunned into silence. I make my way to the front door, where I encounter the roommate with the painted nails having an argument with an Indian takeaway delivery person. The roommate with the painted nails waves to me and winks.

'Was everything to your satisfaction, sir?' he asks. I assume he's being sarcastic. He extends the painted fingernails. 'I'm Madame Darryl. Your hostess for this evening. You are welcome to leave me a tip.'

I feel outraged yet I fumble in my wallet. Madame Darryl is distracted by the takeaway person so without producing my wallet I move into the hallway and speed off, glad that for once I've not been shamed or bullied into a gesture I would later bitterly resent.

I quickly make my way back to the street where I hail the first cab and give them my home address. A minute later my feeling of stunned horror leaves me. I am clutching something which I remember is Jerry's business card. It reads 'Jerry The Sex Pig. No fetish too perverted. Available for home/hotel/foreign travel.' With a shudder I throw it out the window.

I am now back at home, writing in my journal. I have had a thorough shower. I sit, wet, in my toweling robe that Alison purchased for me on my 70th birthday last year. When I remember this my body starts to shake. My God. What would Alison say if she could see me? What story would I make up about my evening? What hundred hells has she been protecting me from, all these years we've been together? I move to my study, where are displayed in their complementary silver frames a clutch of pictures of us together, starting with our wedding picture and moving through our decades together, to the last one, taken in the garden last August.

I must be mad. I should listen to my friends when they tell me grief unhinges the mind. I'm not homosexual. And looking at Alison in the various photos, in a variety of charming poses, I can see now what everyone has always seen. That she's a delightful woman. Pretty. Well-attired. A fitting consort. I sit down in my chair and gather my robe together for comfort. What have I lost? What insanity have I been telling myself? How am I going to get through the days from now?

Four. JERRY and DARRYL and ZAC

Clearing a space among the detritus on the kitchen table so he can put down a cup of coffee, Darryl flexes his fingers and admires his polished nails. Then with a sigh he expertly removes the false nails, enjoying the tiny click they make as he snaps them off. He efficiently scraps the nails into a pile, then glances at the rubbish bin which is overflowing. He sighs and abandons the pile of shiny plastic nails as there is a knock on the door. He jumps up and moves to answer it.

Standing in the cold morning air is Zac. His hair has been clumsily dyed dirty blond, his leather jacket is too big and accidentally torn, his trouser legs have deliberate holes. His face is pasty white yet his eyes gleam with eternal innocence and there is a certain type of man on whom the whole mess works.

Darryl reports laconically 'You look like you've come straight from a night of nameless orgies and class A drugs.' Zac agrees affably and follows him back to the kitchen.

'Is Jerry up?'

Darryl turns his head and screams in the general direction of Jerry's room. 'Jerry! Your love life's here!'

Zac puts a hand on Darryl's arm and says, unexpectedly shyly, 'I'm not really his love life. He's just a guy I like.'

Darryl tucks an arm around Zac and leads him to the kitchen's only chair not covered in ancient newspapers and magazines. 'Do me a favour?' asks Darryl. 'Get him to take a bath and wash his sheets? The vermin are complaining.'

Jerry and Darryl occupy a one-bedroom flat in Jerry's name. The larger sitting room is Darryl's boudoir while the smaller bedroom reeks of Jerry. They share the kitchen and bathroom and have never been known to purchase household cleanser although Darryl has a fetish about personal cleanliness and clean bedding, so he does work the washing machine. Darryl selects the least encrusted coffee cup and makes Zac an instant brew. Zac sits and sips it carefully, his bush-baby eyes glued to Jerry's closed door.

There is a silence because Zac can never think of what to talk to Darryl about other than Jerry, and Darryl has banned that subject. He suddenly brightens and stands.

'Have you seen my butt plug?'

Darryl asks, deadpan, 'No, where did you leave it?

Zac pauses, again exposing an underlying lack of confidence.

'Uh, it's in my butt?' Darryl smiles and Zac swiftly undoes his trousers. Underneath he wears a metal device which begins as a ring around his penis, and then has a smooth metal bar curving under the genitals to join with a metal butt plug on the other end.

'You see it's a ring and a plug' explains Zac patiently.

Darryl ponders the device then asks 'How does it make you feel?'

'Incredible. It's like I'm aware of my arse all the time.'

'It looks like someone's bent a telephone pole and stuck it up you. I can't imagine it's very healthy. What would happen if you fell over? Would it be permanently attached?'

Zac frowns and considers the question seriously. 'I don't know. I got it last night. In exchange for a blow job.'

Darryl sighs and moves to Zac. He pats Zac's bleached hair and Zac pulls up his pants. 'I can't wait to model it for Jerry 'says Zac.

'Child 'answers Darryl. 'You're trying to do all your growing up in a heartbeat. Enjoy your youth. There's lots of time for metal butt plugs and cock rings when you can't get it up anymore.'

Zac is crestfallen. 'I'm not so young, I'm nineteen.'

Darryl throws him an Auntie Mame look. 'Don't be old before your time. Believe me, there's plenty of time to be decrepit.'

Zac tightens his belt and waits. 'I guess I'll see if Jerry's ready to wake up' he says and Darryl nods.

'Be my guest. I have to be at work in half an hour anyway.'

Zac points to the pile of discarded plastic nails. 'Won't you need these?'

'Honey 'responds Darryl, 'I'm a maintenance worker in a hotel. At work I have to be dead butch.'

Zac thinks this is funny and laughs. Then he opens Jerry's door and eagerly enters, unmindful of the stupefying stink. He pulls at the mismatched curtains and one opens, the other is wedged shut. With the slight increase of light that tiptoes, as though ashamed, into the room, he can make out the general shape of his beloved, lying in a stupor on the bed. Jerry's mouth is open, he snores gently. Zac strips out of his clothes and quietly gets into bed with Jerry. He cuddles closer, trying to bridge the gap between their two bodies. Suddenly from Jerry a deep rumble. 'If you snuggle any closer you'll have me on the floor.'

'Morning! Are you glad to see me?'

Jerry lets loose a yawn of stale breath and liquor. 'No. Leave me alone.'

Zac laughs happily and snuggles closer. He gathers Jerry's sleepy genitals gently in his hand. 'Wait till you see what I'm wearing.'

There is a pause and then Jerry's hand finds Zac's face and pushes him off the bed.

'Leave my junk alone' says Jerry. 'I get paid for being molested.'

On the floor, Zac is not sure what's happening. He's no stranger to rough sex but he can't read Jerry's mood. He decides to model the new equipment. He gets back on the bed and sits on Jerry's face. Instantly there's a bellow of indignation and Zac again feels himself being thrown off the bed. He hits the floor with a bang and utters a cry of genuine pain as his steel-enhanced genitals slam the hard wood. The noise brings Darryl, who has changed into his blue boiler suit for work.

'What the fuck! Are you hurting this child!'

Jerry snarls as he throws a pillow in Darryl's direction. 'Get the little shit out of here. I'm trying to sleep.'

Darryl looks to Zac. Zac's eyes are full of tears.

'Don't cry, darling' says Darryl sympathetically.

'I have to. I think I just crushed my nut sack.'

'Get out and don't come back later' snarls Jerry.

'But Jerry, I thought we were an item. You told me you had feelings for me.'

'I lied. You bore me. Piss off.'

Darryl gathers Zac's clothes and the two leave Jerry's bedroom as Jerry, with an indignant howl, turns his back on them and the waking world. In the tiny hallway Darryl watches as Zac painfully dresses.

'Cheer up. You'll get over him. There are other men.'

Zac's tears flow freely. 'Yeah but they don't make me feel like Jerry does.'

'What, overwhelmed by the stench of smegma?'

'What's smegma?'

'Just keep down there regularly washed and you'll never need to know. I'm late. Can I walk you to the tube?'

Zac hesitates. 'Maybe I'll hang around till Jerry's feeling better?'

'Sweetheart, Jerry is a douche. He doesn't deserve you. Also he doesn't want you. But you'll find someone, perhaps someone just as smelly but infinitely kinder to you.'

The two begin their way to the tube station.

'What have you got on the cards today?' Darryl asks.

Zac replies 'I'm doing a regular at 12 noon. And I'll have my mobile on so there'll be others calling on the off chance.'

'That's how to cure a broken heart. Service to others.'

'Yeah.'

The two men enter the tube and split into different directions. Darryl can see Zac wants to add one final thought, so he waits for it.

'Thing is, I thought Jerry and I really had a connection. He's a masseur. I'm a masseur. We could have opened a whole massage parlour.'

'Sounds terrifying' says Darryl warmly. 'And honey, can you rethink the metal appendage? You're too young to be rushed to A & E with a ruptured back passage.'

'Yeah, I have to say it feels really bruised. I'll take some cough mixture when I get home.'

'Wouldn't paracetamol be more effective?'

'If I take cough mixture with paracetamol it's a bigger buzz.'

Darryl laughs. 'Ah, those innocent days of paracetamol washed down with vodka. I can't take tablets anymore, it's something I vowed in N.A.'

Darryl leans down to embrace Zac then disappears swiftly, waving one hand behind him like Liza Minnelli as Sally Bowles at the end of *Cabaret.* Zac has not seen *Cabaret* and does not get the allusion, but he still laughs and waves.

A while later, back at the flat, Jerry finally rises. He sniffs under his armpits and decides he can go without for another day. He checks his mobile and has three missed calls who have left messages. He stands naked in the kitchen, reusing Zac's coffee cup, while listening to his messages. One is pornographic and begins promisingly then deteriorates into grunts, so he kills it. The second he calls back and makes an appointment with for later. The third is an elderly voice, formal, rather distressed. Saying something about a valuable watch which he left in Jerry's room. Jerry kills that call as well and returns to his room. He finds the watch. A *Cartier* with a proper sapphire bezel and a lizard strap. He straps it to his wrist and returns to the kitchen. Grubbing inside the encrusted fridge he locates the remains of last night's curry which he eats standing up, cold.

Five. ALEC

Travelling into work by taxi gives Alec ample time to regret his actions of the previous evening. Leaving his watch was the last straw. Although he has left a detailed message, he is by no means confident that the man will return his call. The watch has sentimental as well as monetary value.' Alison bought it for him and although it was of course his money she spent days finding the perfect strap and having it engraved. Alec looks moodily out of the window, his eyes automatically scanning the young men on the pavement. Then he remembers that he's not gay after all and drags his attention onto the passing women.

Entering the splendid offices that serve as headquarters for Bland & Partners, the family firm, he receives a beaming smile from Jenny at reception. Conscious of his new determination to rejoin the ranks of heterosexual workers he smiles back and as he takes his morning paper says gallantly:

'Good morning, Jenny. I must say you look particularly pert-breasted this morning. Unconscious of the wake of raised eyebrows and sudden breath intakes he leaves in his wake, Alec ascends to the second floor and shuts himself in his plush office. He gets on with the serious business of shifting the papers in his in-tray into three categories. By the time he's finished he can't remember which pile is 'urgent', which 'hold 'and which 'discard 'so he rings for his PA and asks her to do it for him. A little while later there's a discreet knock on his door and Dennis enters.

'Morning old – Morning Alec. Must say we weren't expecting to see you today.'

It is true that when Alec was under the apprehension that he would be spending time exploring his homosexual inclinations he intimated he would be in the office less. His plans having changed he stares at Dennis. Why on earth would he be anywhere other than at work?

'Oh fine 'says Dennis. 'Only I spent a day reorganising your meetings et cetera. Do you want to take them back now?'

Alec considers. 'I believe my only chance for happiness in life from now is in giving service to others.'

Dennis frowns. He had hoped the old boy would hardly be around so he could continue infiltrating his own men into the company. It appears another plan will need to be pursued.

'That's great, Alec. I'm sure we still need you.'

'I would think so' says Alec, but with a hint of elderly steel. 'It's still my company. I know when Alison got sick I had to take my foot off the accelerator but now I'm back, in the driver's seat so to say, I expect to double revenue. Which will require new directions so let's get some thinking going regarding expansion.'

Inwardly Dennis groans. The last thing he needs is speculative operations. He's perfectly happy with working hard enough to make good money, without selling his soul to the company. Some people enjoy their home life.

Alec glances at his watch and grunts as he again remembers that he left it at the bedside of a male sex worker. Just the thought makes him blush and he's pleased when Rochelle, his PA, enters and reminds him of a newly inserted meeting. As Rochelle, efficient in everything, closes the door Alec makes a head gesture in her direction.

'Good looking woman, that.'

Rochelle is in her mid-40s and wears support stockings for early varicose veins. She would be grateful to hear she has a fan.

‘Yes? Says Dennis, who always believed Rohelle was hired for her lack of looks, since it was unlikely anyone would come between her and putting in a 70-hour week.

‘Damn fine’ mutters Alec, pleased that Dennis is around to hear, and doubtless to pass on to others, that Alec is in the market for a new woman.

Back in his own office Dennis sees Vice Head of Production Sandra’s head peering round the door frame and beckons her in.

Sandra’s eyes gleam malevolently. ‘Just a quick heads up. Alec apparently just told reception she had particularly pert breasts this morning.’

Dennis blinks. ‘He just told me Rochelle is a good-looking woman. And then he said damn fine.’

They stare at each other. ‘He’s gone sex mad' is Sandra’s opinion.

‘He’s still the Chairman’ Dennis reminds her.

‘Can I trust that I’ll be safe alone with him? ’asks Sandra. ‘Lots of men get married in their seventies’. Both are aware of the many secretive meetings they have shared while plotting their takeover of Alec’s family business. ‘What if he starts a new family?’

‘Don’t panic. Don’t forget he still looks like a walrus missing his ice flow.’

‘Some women find that sort of thing strangely arousing’ muses Sandra.

‘Don’t do that!’

‘What?’

‘You’ve just fluffed your hair.’

‘I did not! I just remarked …’

'And then you fluffed your hair. Are you telling me you find Alec strangely arousing?'

Sandra sends Dennis an extremely dirty look.

'Fine, then' says Dennis. 'Let's just concentrate on keeping the damage to a minimum. Unless we can get him kicked out on sexual grounds' he concludes on a hopeful note.

On Tuesday Alec again motors by taxi into work, carefully shifting his eyes from men to women. He strides into his building and suddenly realises that, after his kind words to Jenny the previous day, he'd better say something else. He wouldn't want her thinking he found fault with her appearance this morning. Fortunately she is wearing a striking blouse, teamed with fuschia lipstick. Fixing her with a basilisk stare he announces in ringing tones 'I see you've rouged your lips. Very becoming. I would imagine a hue similar to your nipples.' Pleased with this spontaneous compliment he proceeds to his office, unaware of the wave of horror washing behind him.

On Thursday Alec remembers in time to think up something thoughtful in the taxi. For some unknown reason, thinks Alec, Jenny is looking rather wary this morning. Probably to do with all these people milling around, for it is unusual to see so many people standing casually around in reception. Alec has again pre-chosen a compliment for Jenny but when he sees her outfit he drops it. She is concealed behind a thick Aran sweater. Thinking of mountains gives Alec his cue. 'This morning you remind me of the mountains of Mourne. Twin peaks. You know, the ones that sweep down to the sea.' As he moves off to his office he is aware of a hot buzz of conversation behind him but he isn't a man to return and make unnecessary enquiries.

On Friday Jenny calls in sick and H.R. organises an emergency replacement. When Alec arrives and pushes his way through the throng he discovers that rather than Jenny there is a young man at reception. Biracial, tall and slender, with extraordinary amber eyes and skin like tawny gold. Alec bolts past without even a cursory greeting, thereby disappointing the expectant throng.

Friday evening and Alec settles himself into the comfortable chair opposite Guy.

He begins 'I'm terribly sorry, I'm wasting your valuable time.'

Guy says nothing, merely increasing his look of polite interest a few percentage points.

'Yes, you see I think it's the grief. I don't think I'm homosexual. So I don't need to come here anymore.'

Guy nods. What he's thinking is that this reaction to early therapy is common. The person, having found the courage to attend in the first place then loses their nerve and wants to pretend that everything is sorted. It's called 'the flight into health.' The fact that there is a term for it in the therapy profession indicates how often the phenomenon occurs. Guy does not say any of this, instead he smiles encouragingly, to tempt Alec to elucidate further on his decision.

'So, thank you for your efforts.'

This is disappointing for Guy, but therapists have to be tough. Like all freelancers they roll with the punches. Oh well, it's not as though Ted is moving out tomorrow, thinks Guy. And it's not Alec's problem. You learn early in therapy training that the only things you can expect from your client is that they turn up on time and pay you. Everything else is on the therapist's docket.

After a silence Alec adds 'So I don't have anything to say.'

Guy speaks. 'These sessions are fifty minutes. That's your time. If you really don't have anything to say, if you feel uncomfortable sitting in silence, you can end the session whenever you wish.'

After a moment Alec rises carefully from his chair and reaches for his wallet. He pays the fee for the session and moves to the front door.

'Thank you again' he says as he opens the door and exits. Guy takes the money and adds it to the little pile in his desk drawer. After a moment Ted comes out of the bedroom.

'That didn't last long. Did you frighten them off?'

'No. He didn't need me.'

'Huh. I'm not trying to therapise you but how did that feel?'

'Meaning?'

'I wonder if it's the same way I've been feeling?'

Guy is conscious that he is not ready for another break up in the same evening.

'I don't know what you mean.'

In response Ted thrusts his mobile phone towards Guy. 'What do you think of this bloke?'

Guy recognises the logo of gay dating app. Grindr. A pleasant-looking man, no Marvel Superhero, smiles out of a slightly blurred photo.

'He looks okay. Are you trying to tell me something?'

'I thought I'd meet up with him this evening, maybe grab a coffee or see a movie.'

Ted then walks back to their bedroom and Guy registers that he's dressed for going out. His mouth tightens. He calls 'So you're not organising dinner tonight?'

For a moment there is silence then Ted returns wearing a jacket, clutching his house keys.

'No. I realise you're a better cook than me but it's been me every night. And I'm getting bored with my own selections.'

Guy nods and mutters 'I can't blame you.'

Ted checks his hair in the mirror next to the front door. He shakes it up, then tidies the disheveled result. Guy watches, remembering how he used to love taking his fingers to Ted's wild mop, gently untangling the mass of unruly curls. Now Ted wears his hair short so shaking and tidying is more of a habit, producing little discernible difference.

'Call me when you're on your way back.'

Ted looks into the mirror and speaks to Guy's reflection.

'I might forget. Don't wait up.'

Ted turns around and Guy doesn't move. The two men regard each other unhappily .

'Enjoy the film. What are you going to see?'

This deliberate politeness, Ted knows, is Guy's way of expressing anger.

He says 'If you don't want me to go, I won't.'

Guy considers this for a moment. He slowly shakes his head. 'I don't want to get in the way of you having a good time.'

'You can say something. I mean we live together. You have a right to expect me to be here.'

Guy again thinks carefully before replying. 'We're not married, remember?'

Ted's mouth twists spitefully. 'Yeah, now I understand why you were so insistent. 'We love each other totally already, Ted, we don't have to ape heterosexuals to be completely happy'.'

'We do own this place together' Guy reminds him.

'Yes but why does that feel like another piece of crap to get sorted out, rather than security?'

Guy nods. 'It's only an evening at the movies. If it was one of your girlfriends, we wouldn't even be having this conversation.'

Ted stands, peering with two round eyes of misery at his partner.

'But it's not. And the truth is you really don't care.'

Guy sighs deeply. 'I'm sorry if you're looking for a fight. I'm respecting your right to whatever you need.'

Ted shakes his head angrily. 'You're using your training against me. When are you going to be honest? When are you going to tell me you just don't love me anymore? I don't know why you've stopped loving me. Believe me my feelings for you haven't changed at all!'

Guy thinks and nods. 'So, it's just a movie? Nothing for me to worry about.'

Ted sighs in frustration. He's aware that what should have been a powerful statement from him has been undercut by Guy's evident lack of interest. He gasps. 'This is what my father used to do. I'd need something from him and he wouldn't give it to me. You bastard. You piece of shit. You know I hate it when you shrug and walk away. You know that's what *he* always did!'

Guy's expression doesn't change. 'I also know you might hate me if I stopped you having a good time.'

Ted's eyes fill with tears. 'You *know* I don't want to go out with some online bloke. You know I want us to get married!'

Guy moves back to the sitting room and sits down. Ted follows, standing behind Guy's chair. Guy speaks quietly. 'And *you* know I have my own boundaries. We're already far too far down the straight road just buying this place together. If you've been hanging around in the hope I'll put a ring on your third finger left hand you're only going to be even more disappointed.'

Ted jangles his keys. 'Fine. I'm off out. If I'm not back by the morning just be glad I'm having a good time for once.'

Guy waits for the inevitable slam of the front door. When it comes he exhales. He opens a cold beer and drinks it from the bottle.

'Looks like we've broken up' he says to the empty air. 'Now all the rest is paperwork.'

He reaches for the remote, then stops. Nine years is a long time. Worthwhile years of good work, taking the raw material of Ted, his insecurities and sorrows, and setting him on the path to adulthood. If only Ted understood that Guy really has no more to give him. This is what Guy is. He's a carer. He's a healer. The sad truth is after the healing he sees no further purpose in a relationship. However, now that Ted seems to have reached the point where he is beginning to look outward, the possibility opens that Guy will also be able to look around. Who knows whom he will light on? The prospect of a new man, a new challenge, fills Guy with intense excitement.

Yes, he thinks, like Ted I could pick someone off Grindr. Yet that would be too easy. I prefer to see what the wind blows my way. Perhaps next time I'll look for someone with artistic ambitions.

Someone who will never be secure and stable. I'll always have to be there, to patch them up, to listen to their self-doubts and inner terrors. The thought restores Guy's equilibrium and for the rest of the evening, spent watching T.V. and drinking beers from the bottle, he gives hardly a thought to Ted. And when he does, it's principally about how they're going to deal with dividing the flat.

Six. ALEC

Before Alec can drive out to his former sister-in-law Rebecca's country home for the weekend, he has business to attend to in the office. He is aware that during the months of Alison's worsening health he too often let matters drift, he was too quick to delegate important decisions to others. He's not a fool, he's aware that his position as MD and Chairman is always under threat. One thing his father taught him is that in business everyone's your friend and colleague till they're your enemy. So ignore the first stage and cut to the bottom line. Some employers like to tell their workers that the company is one big happy family, but Alec's personal experience of the family left him so wounded that he prefers to keep a distance between himself and his workers. By never confusing work and family he avoids the inevitable heartache that follows suddenly receiving someone's letter of resignation. When one comes it takes a mere nanosecond before he adjusts to what it will mean to go on each working day without that particular person.

It's part of what his two closest colleagues, Dennis and Sandra, find difficult about working at Bland's. They would like to call him Uncle Alec while they're backstabbing and accruing sufficient votes to get rid of the old nuisance. They'd like him to be the kind of genial old gink who would waffle for a bit in meetings then fall into a refreshing sleep. For a while, when Alison was sinking, they nursed the hope that he would take her death as a signal to retire. They've been monitoring his work hours and, to their dismay, he's behaving like a junior employee with something to prove.

Since Alec has never been around a family where trust and support were on offer it doesn't worry him that the trust and support he receives from his colleagues is strictly for surface show. In fact he wouldn't appreciate the deeper sort, it would only make him extra wary and suspicious. Alison was a good wife in that when she saw she was not going to have a happy and fulfilled emotional and sexual life she found other ways of occupying herself. Thinking about Alison at the office, though, is not an activity Alec wants to encourage in himself.

Conscious that his spending the weekend with Alison's sister will cut down his ability to focus on work, Alec disregards lunch and even tea breaks to shift as much paperwork as possible. His poor PA, Rochelle, feels swamped. Regarding her Alec can't quite put his finger on it, but she's somehow changed. The fact is that having heard through the grapevine that Alec believes she is a good-looking woman, Rochelle now feels obligated to drop the support stockings. And people have been very complimentary, saying they can hardly see the varicose veins. So she's twinned the bare leg look with frocks that Alec can only describe as 'booby dresses'. It's made her rather formidable, like Margaret Thatcher with cleavage.

Alec needs someone to book him a taxi but he feels bad about asking Rochelle so he remembers he can book one at reception. Jenny is always willing. Alec trots off to reception, and too late remembers that Jenny is off sick and there is a young man behind the desk. Alec can feel his face flushing bright scarlet and his stammering is adding to his confusion.

'Yes sir?' asks the vision behind the desk. Alec remembers that he is not homosexual and therefore he can speak to this young man with perfect composure.

'A-a-a- - can – can you – can you please. Uh. A taxi. For six thirty this evening.'

'Yes sir. And where should I say you want to go?'

'Well it's obvious, I want to go – to go to – to Rebecca's. Didn't I explain that?'

The young man sighs patiently. Prior to accepting the post he was warned there was an elderly man who was difficult. ‘No, sir. Do you have Rebecca’s address?’ There’s a silence from the other end of the conversation so the temporary receptionist stands up and peers over the glass partition. Alec is painfully aware that the young man is wearing a very tight shirt, one that hugs and caresses every knotted muscle of his torso.

‘Yhhh… what’s your name?’

‘I’m Seymon.’

‘Seymour?’

‘No sir. Seymon. It’s French.’

Alec stares for another moment before he realises he’s been going about this all wrong. It’s not that he finds Seymon irresistible, it’s more that he finds himself unable to remember any details of Rebecca’s address. Even coming up with the name Rebeca was a stretch.

‘Uh … Yes, French’ says Alec, holding onto the last comment from the vision. He knows he needs to end the discussion, he’s aware that several people have stopped and cannot help listening.

‘I suppose you’ll be going back there, now. I mean back to the other side of the channel.’

To his horror Seymon clearly takes this as a personal attack. ‘Sir, I have dual citizenship. I have lived in the UK for the last 15 years!’

‘Yes, of course, so sorry, just wondered – welcome to the company ‘. Alec bolts. He leaves a chorus of raised eyebrows, cynical smiles and a clutch of employees all looking forward to spreading the news that the old boy is not only a sexist, he’s also xenophobic. Seymon shakes his beautiful head and goes back to what he was doing, which was using the reception computer to write to his mother in Chartres. Now he has something specific about the fascist English to add.

Alec prevails upon Rochelle to organise his taxi. She's done it before so needs no explaining. Alec does think it odd that when Rochelle comes into his office to confirm the arrangements she leans heavily over his desk. Without wishing to pry Alec can clearly see that Rochelle is either not wearing a bra or wearing one that lifts and separates her breasts. He expects she has a big evening planned.

As Rochelle leaves for the evening, she checks her make-up and hair in a pocket-sized mirror. Removing a lunchtime shred of corn from an incisor she takes the letters for signing she has prepared and knocks on Alec's door before entering. He smiles at her and she bends over his desk heavily as she deposits the letters.

'Just off, Mr Bland.'

'Thank you. I'll sign those on Monday.'

'I can wait and post them on the way out if you like?'

'No, I want to think about these over the weekend. Delicate negotiations, you know.'

Rochelle nods. She loves her job, it makes her feel close to the centre of power.

'Enjoy your big night' says Alec, suddenly feeling light-hearted.

Rochelle stops. All she's doing is going home to a cold flat and a warm cat.

'I'm not doing anything special' she responds.

'Oh. I thought you – oh, never mind' says Alec.

Rochelle nods and leaves Alec's office. On her face is a happy smile. He *has* noticed.

Driving to the country by taxi is an extravagance but Alec writes it off to expenses and since it's his family business what difference does it make? He likes black cabs, they remind him of an earlier, simpler world. And he likes the look of wonder on the faces at the other side, since there are so many other cheaper ways of travelling. He's looking to present an air of casual luxury, of someone for whom money simply is no object, at least when it comes to transport. He is blissfully unaware that most people consider him hopelessly out of touch with the new, cost-efficient ways of travelling.

'Rebecca' he says as he sees her coming out of her house to greet him. He suddenly remembers he meant to bring some wine for dinner. Never mind, Rebecca won't expect it.

The tense smile Rebeca wears becomes even more pronounced when she sees that once again Alec has not brought any gifts. No flowers, no wine. Nothing that acknowledges the hospitality he will expect in full measure over the next 18 hours. However, Rebecca is aware that she already has things to tell the old boy, so she merely chalks up 'ungrateful skinflint' to the list. She finds it particularly irksome that he spends so much money on a black cab when he knows she would pick him up from the station. They could then split the difference.

Alec looks around Rebecca's guest room with satisfaction. She's upgraded the bureau from the Ikea-purchase old one to a charming antique bureau of which he can approve. And since he was the one who frequently dropped little hints to Rebecca that the bureau let the whole room down, he's pleased to see she's taken his feedback. He pats the new bureau approvingly.

Downstairs Rebecca is making snacks and glaring up at the ceiling in the direction of the guest room. 'I bet he won't even notice' she mutters to her husband. Billy prides himself on being implacable, so he merely smiles implacably and nods. 'Five hundred pounds I paid for that bureau' adds Rebecca.

'I know' says Billy soothingly. 'In fact, I was the one who paid the credit card.'

'And if he does notice he won't say anything. People like him with all their money expect everyone feels the same as them. And taking a taxi all the way from London!'

Billy's glad Alec has asked to stay only one night. Even *his* equilibrium has limits.

'I'm sure he'll notice even if it's only subconsciously.'

'Ha! He doesn't *have* a subconscious!'

Over drinks and snacks Rebecca waits and silently fumes. Finally she can bear it no longer. 'Did you notice the lovely antique bureau in the guest room?'

Lulled by a warm fire and a stream of inconsequential chatter Alec has fallen into a reverie and takes a moment to realise a direct question has been asked.

'What? Oh yes. I noticed.'

'Cost us five hundred pounds' says Rebecca grimly. Alec winces. He was always taught that speaking of money is vulgar and even though Rebecca is only fifteen years younger than him she was evidently brought up differently. He wonders what the etiquette should be. All he can remember is that if money is mentioned, however much you have, you should always behave as though it was entirely without importance. Even make a joke of it.

'Really?' he says gallantly. 'You were robbed!'

Alec stands, unaware that the sharp intake of breath he just heard was not from the dog but from the hostess.

'I'll just use the facilities' he says as he moves away, gliding swiftly like a walrus getting wind of a shoal of herring in the next bay.

Billy hears a noise like air rushing from a punctured inner tube and knows that once again his wife is containing herself by breathing out very slowly but audibly.

'It's only for one night. He is your brother-in-law.'

'Keep telling me that. I'm going to need it' says Rebecca grimly as she exits to the kitchen.

To prepare for Alec's overnight stay, Billy has prepared a number of consoling phrases to drop into the conversation. He needs only a cue from Alec, possibly something about how quiet the house is without her. Or how Alec often calls out to her and again realises she's gone. With such a cue Billy could lay a truly awesome cliché on the table. But Alec gives him no opening. Instead Alec, when he can be prevailed upon to talk about anything, mutters in a desultory way about work. As the often silent dinner proceeds Rebecca is aware that her patience is becoming more and more frayed. She just wants him to say one unkind or thoughtless word about her late sister and he will regret it.

But no such opener comes from Alec. He talks a little of the journey, and his intention of really taking the reins at the office. He even asks if Rebecca knows what he means by the expression 'booby dress', which she doesn't.

Finally Rebecca decides that she must either forcibly bring up the subject or throw herself across the table and slap the offending party.

'It must be very different without Alison.'

Alec was in the middle of negotiating the last strawberry from the strawberry cheesecake onto his spoon. His hand shakes as the strawberry meets its fate. He puts down the spoon.

'Of course. You must know, though, that Alison and I … well we didn't spend much time together. I think she preferred it.'

Rebecca is so incensed, so immediately protective of her maligned late sister, so entirely caught up in an inner fury of rage that she is temporarily incapable of coherent speech. Instead she again begins to whistle through her teeth. Billy, picking up on the danger sign, seeks to pour oil on troubled waters in his calming way.

'There's so much to adjust to.'

Alec considers this while licking his spoon angelically. 'Or not. You see, all that's been taken away is that concern when I come in the front door at night that she's had a bad day. Now I know she's not had any day at all it's really much simpler. I just come home, put the bath on, see what's on the telly and an hour later I'm eating whatever's in the fridge and watching some bit of rubbish.'

'While my sister lies literally in ashes' says Rebecca.

Alec looks at her with surprise. 'Yes, that's why we had her cremated. I couldn't decide what to do with the urn. Should I leave it in the front hall, or would that carry the danger of being knocked over? Or should I put it on her bedside table? Finally I put her in the cupboard until a really good place occurred to me.'

The moment Rebecca had been waiting for has arrived.

'In. The. Cupboard?!' she asks as three separate, venomous accusations. '*You put my late sister in the cupboard!?"*

'Only so someone wouldn't knock her over' explains Billy soothingly.

'You – you appalling, heartless monster!' Harsh words, yes, and accompanied by Rebecca leaping up so recklessly that her chair flies back and smashes against a plant stand, dislodging the plant and spewing earth and fern over the carpet.

'You destroyed my sister!'

'Now that's not technically true' says Billy, on the floor and scooping the earth back into the shattered Arts & Crafts terracotta pot.

'Shut up Billy!' howls the discombobulated hostess. From her vantage point Rebecca turns an accusing finger on Alec.

'If you knew how many nights Alison was on the phone to me! The tears! The grief! Night after night she would hear you come home, go into your study, emerge only to go into your bedroom. The nights she would call out, asking you to come to say goodnight. All she got would be a knock on her door and a 'Goodnight Alison.' You think she died of cancer? She died of neglect! I wish there was a law about destroying people through unkindness because I would have you prosecuted to the full extent of the law!'

Alec is stunned and silent for a moment. Then he speaks.

'Is this about the bureau? I only meant to compliment you. Perhaps five hundred pounds was a very good price indeed.'

Rebecca stamps her foot on the carpet, something Billy thought happened only in West End drawing room comedies.

'*It's not about the- fucking - bureau!!!* I begged her to leave you! She wouldn't! She said she would stay loyal to you for the whole of her life! Even when she was dying, she preferred to stay in that fridge you call a home.'

Alec isn't often roused to defend himself. Having grown up with an autocratic father who punished all rebellion severely, then married to a woman who turned martyrdom into a full-time vocation he has always taken the silent road. But even Alec can be stirred into defensive action.

‘I do not recognise myself in your description. I did my best by your sister. I was also loyal to her. I was almost obliterated when our son was born helplessly compromised. I knew how guilty she felt. So even though I had many, many reasons for wanting to leave myself, I stayed loyal to Alison.’

Rebecca gasps. This is truly a different angle. ‘What do you mean, you had many reasons for leaving yourself. From your side you had the perfect marriage. An entirely obliging, selfless wife who always sacrificed herself in your best interests.’

‘My best interests!’ Alec thunders. ‘Do you have any – do you have *any idea* what I have suffered over these years? Do you know what it was like to stand on one side of the road and watch the life I could have lived taking place on the other side and not be able to cross over?’

‘Rubbish’ says Rebecca automatically. ‘You’re just feeling sorry for yourself.’

‘I have a right to feel sorry for myself!’ thunders Alec.

‘Perhaps not so loud’ comments Billy. ‘The neighbours will hear.’

‘I don’t give a toss!’ snaps Alec.

‘Shut up Billy, we’re the only house for half a mile’ adds his wife. Having had a moment when they were united against Billy, the two then face each other off again.

‘I never liked or approved of you’ says Rebecca, inwardly thrilled at the opportunity to at last speak her piece. ‘I begged her not to marry you. I said you were a dried-up piece of formalised conservative exploitation who would never appreciate or understand her.’

Alec's eyes bulge dangerously. 'You think you are sharing secrets? You think I haven't always known that your surface friendship hid only your duplicity?'

Rebecca always prided herself on concealing her true feelings. Now she realises that she could have saved a lot of internal anguish. The old buzzard never appreciated it.

'The truth is you married my sister on a lie. You said you would honour and love her forever. You promised to protect and care for her. Instead, you drove her from health and security to a miserable and painful death. Your lie is your fate. You will forever carry the shame and guilt of what you've done.'

Billy is secretly impressed with his wife's range of insult, and also her focused delivery. Too often one has something really unpleasant to impart but gets tangled up in irrelevancies. Rebecca, however, has had many years to hone her attack.

'The only thing anyone ever liked about you was my sister. The only reason you were tolerated in civilised society is you were with Alison. The only Christmas cards you ever received were always to Alison and Alec and believe me many people would have left your name off if it wasn't for the fact that it would have hurt Alison! Who you continuously hurt in so many, many ways! It's no secret, Alec. And if you want to know whether or not I'm telling the truth – just wait till Christmas! Just wait till you're the only house in the road the postman never visits. Because no one loves you, Alec! No one is happy to see you! No one cares!'

Up till now Alec has been on the receiving end of Rebecca's tirade from the comfort of his chair. Now he stands and moves to a convenient spot on the wall. He rests his aching back against the cool brick.

'I am aware that no one cares, Rebecca' he says quietly.

'Don't try that, you've always been the centre of your own universe. You always think you're bigger and better than other people!'

Alec thinks through the truth of this remark before continuing. 'Yes, I can see that's how I must appear to the world. When someone's in my work position, both powerful and also vulnerable, I have always had to project an image of being above the rest. It's been my defence.'

'That's interesting' says Billy in a reconciling tone.

'Rubbish' snaps Rebecca. 'You manipulate. You manipulated my sister. You manipulate your employees. You're like every bully I've ever met. When they're cornered, suddenly they start the self-pity.'

Alec rubs his back against the wall. A little further along a picture falls to the floor. Billy retrieves it and explains gently that the glass is only cracked, you can hardly see it. However no one hears him because Rebecca is talking.

'I don't know why you decided to marry and destroy my sister. But even you, in all your monstrous ego, must admit that you have *some* responsibility. And your poor son – you couldn't even give my sister healthy sperm! You had to give her sperm as diseased and misshapen as you!'

Billy thinks the evening has gone as far as it can, and further. 'Who's for coffee?' he asks, dropping the damaged picture onto a convenient chair.

'I'm sorry, but you asked for it' says Rebecca. Even she is somehow disturbed by the quality of silence from her brother-in-law. Alec has been staring at the floor. Now he looks up and into Rebecca's flaring eyes.

'Everything you say is true' he says simply. 'It was not what I intended. It was not what I wanted. It's all true. You want to know what the real secret of my marriage to your sister is?'

Billy doesn't. He knows enough to know that it's not going to be a positive one. 'Coffee?' he again urges.

Rebecca, though, fixes Alec with a defiant, flaming stare and nods, deliberately. 'Be my guest.'

'I'm gay. I'm homosexual' says Alec simply, and as he does so his heart leaps into life.

Billy coughs. Rebecca snorts. The fire seems to crackle into unnecessary fury.

'It's true. I married because my father told me it was necessary if I was going to become Chairman. I married Alison because although I never directly told her so, she knew.'

'Lies!' howls Rebecca. 'Lies! You're being deliberately obscene. My sister told me everything. Everything! If she had suspected you were queer she would have told me!'

Now that he has spoken his deepest truth Alec has little to add. With as much dignity as he can muster he moves from the dining room to the sitting room and takes his seat on his usual chair. Followed by a fuming Rebecca and a particularly thoughtful Billy.

'I don't want you sitting in my chairs in my house' says Rebecca.

'Then you shouldn't have invited me to stay overnight' answers Alec, in a neutral tone.

Billy coughs.

Rebecca continues. 'I don't want you in my house a second longer. You've destroyed my sister. Now you've lied to me. I have gay friends and they would be insulted that you have tried to use their situation to cover your own disgusting failures with my sister.'

Billy coughs again.

'You are the worst person I have ever met. For heaven's sake, Billy, if your throat is tickling drink some water.'

'I'm coughing to draw your attention' he says mildly. 'The thing is, Alison confided in me.'

Rebecca turns on her husband like a snake turning on a rabbit. A rabbit who, it turns out, has been concealing vital information. 'What?!'

'She never wanted you to know. I think she thought you wouldn't handle it very well. But Alec's right, Alison told me several times, over the years, that she believed her husband was gay.'

Rebecca knows that in the morning she will have the mother of migraines. However she's not ready to quit the battlefield.

'Then if that's true, why did the two of you stay together? Why did she literally die of unhappiness?' she howls.

From Alec there is a sigh, anguished enough to melt the hearts of The Weird Sisters from The Scottish Play.

'Who knows why any of us do anything?' he asks philosophically. 'I think if I'd been younger, if our son hadn't been born mentally incapacitated, if my father hadn't so terrified me that I never knew what I wanted or who I was …'

'Have you got a boyfriend or something?' asks Rebecca with hostility.

Alec brays a bitter laugh. 'No. I never have. And I can't see it happening now, can you?'

'So what are you going to do, Alec?' asks Billy. An unhappy silence reverberates through the room, disturbing the usual placid country ambiance.

Alec stands, stretches and yawns. 'I'm going to do what I've always done. Go to bed on my own and sleep as well as I can. Tomorrow is another day. I don't expect to see either of you in the morning. Thank you for your hospitality.'

Alec shuffles off, leaving Billy staring at Rebecca. For a moment Rebecca considers hitting him with the picture frame that got cracked yet she is also conscious that his big revelation has trumped anything she can do in return.

'I don't believe he's gay' hisses Rebecca.

Billy shrugs.

'I can't believe she told you and never told me' she continues.

Billy sighs.

'I won't sleep tonight' says Rebecca. 'I'll sleep down here.'

'That's not necessary. I prefer we sleep together' says Billy.

'I'll sleep down here' says Rebecca, somehow satisfied that Billy, who kept such important news from her all these years, will thereby pass a difficult and sleepless night, like her.

Upstairs, pulling the sheets closer around him, Alec reflects on the evening. Of course, that nonsense about him not being gay, that was only the result of that truly stupefying night out. He mustn't do that again. He knows what he is and that's an end to it. Yet he doesn't regret what happened this evening. Finally coming out as who he really is to someone in his life was the most satisfying conversation he can ever remember having. And what was especially rewarding was how neither of the other parties blamed him. Not for actually being gay. Although he could be blamed for his actions in the cover up, he wasn't blamed for what he truly is. He glances at the new antique bureau. When he leaves in the morning, he will leave a cheque to cover its cost along with a note explaining it is a present from him. He raises up on one arm and looks at the carpet. It's pretty thread bare.

He'll round up the figure so Rebecca can also replace the rug. Alec switches off the light. Then he remembers Guy. Presumably he needs to return to Guy and explain that in fact he very definitely is gay, and please to forget what he said on the previous occasion. While composing this speech in his head Alec feels overcome by a wave of deep tiredness. The country always has that effect. So he closes his eyes and for the first time in as long as he can remember he sleeps the whole night through.

Seven. DARRYL AND JERRY

Alone at home after a tiring day at work, Darryl has just enough energy to discard his men's clothes, throw on dolly pyjamas, fluffy slippers and a wig, and glue on simple acrylic nails. Feeling more like himself he makes a cup of soothing Horlicks. While Jerry has been in Gran Canaria Darryl has attempted to tidy and clean the flat. He has got as far as stripping the bed in Jerry's room, washing his bedlinen and straightening out Jerry's curtains. Then faced with the rubbish dump that is the kitchen and the obscenity that is the bathroom he loses focus and when Jerry returns, pulling his wheelie and wearing a checkered hat, he finds Darryl sitting in his usual spot in amongst the detritus that throngs the kitchen table. He grunts a greeting and goes to his bedroom, returning immediately.

'Did someone steal my bed stuff?'

Darryl, who has been miserably contemplating the sink, piled up with dishes, plates and empty cereal packets, suddenly snaps into awareness. 'Right! I washed them. And then I …'

He rushes out the flat and down to the laundromat on the corner. Surely it's been only three days since he shoved Jerry's bedlinen into a machine and hit Heavy Wash. Surely someone will have taken out the linen and left it neatly on top of the machine? It is true that someone has removed the linen but not that it is anywhere to be found. Returning to the flat Darryl shrugs his shoulders at Jerry and goes back to reading the free morning paper.

For a while Jerry says nothing. Then someone calls to set up a massage. This indirect reminder of the missing bedlinen causes Jerry to stop worrying the psoriasis behind his left ear and confront Darryl.

'Where's my bed stuff?'

'Bed linen. I told you. It's being washed.'

'You bloody well left it there, didn't you?'

'I left a post-it explaining when I would return' replies Darryl.

There is a silence and for a moment Darryl is hopeful his quick thinking has saved the day. Jerry turns on his heel and storms out the room. A moment later Darryl hears concerning noises from his own room, noises that sound like possessions being hurtled left and right. With a cry he jumps to his feet and makes for the bedroom where he stands by the door, watching Jerry sweeping the contents of Darryl's make-up table onto the floor.

'Stop! That's expensive!'

'I want you out Darryl. This arrangement isn't working!'

'I'll buy you new sheets, for heaven's sake!'

'Except you don't. You never have the cash.'

'Of course I have cash. I work don't I?'

Jerry inherited the flat on the death of an aunt. Although not blessed with comprehensive financial acumen Jerry has enough native cunning to realise that since the life of a freelance masseur has ups and downs he needs someone with a regular salary to underwrite the flat's ongoing expenses. Darryl presented himself as a man with a paycheck and moved in. It took a while for Jerry to discover the flaw in the arrangement.

'No, you've never got cash! You're thousands in debt. Every month your wages are garnished and any spare cash – you know where it goes? – '

'You're exaggerating. I might be short now and then but I have a regular income!'

Jerry smiles nastily. 'Any cash you have goes in there.' Here he indicates Darryl's battered and ancient laptop. He has named Darryl's weak spot and labelled the elephant in the room.

'I don't spend hardly anything anymore' he says in a soft whine, like Mamie in *Gone with The Wind.*

'Look at you – cricketpoker.com, tennispoker.com, t-girlpoker.com. You're an addict. You should be in therapy or somewhere. You make more money than me and I *know* you get up in the night and eat whatever I've organised for my breakfast. Since you moved in I've lost ten pounds. Some of my clients who like bears are complaining I'm no longer satisfying their fetish!'

'Actually I must say you look good now' says Darryl, honestly impacted by Jerry's 10 days in the sun and sand. 'And the smell has improved. Not, I'm sure, because you've actually been taking baths, but the fresh sea water has cleaned out all your crevices. However that won't last long now you're back in London.'

'I'm a sex pig!' thunders Jerry. 'My public likes me dirty!'

'But I didn't know that when I moved in' says Darryl.

'Yeah, well princess, time to find a new castle. I want you out of here by this time tomorrow. You've got 24 hours.'

Darryl's mouth opens and his face registers distress. He can't help comparing his expression with dear Vivien's when the soldier breaks into Tara, intent on looting and rape. He rather thinks he does a more convincing job of a woman on the edge.

'But I have to live somewhere! I need my work clothes. I have a job!'

'Great so I don't need to worry about you. Not that I would.'

'Jerry, at least give me time to find something suitable.'

'Twenty-four hours then your drag gets turfed out the window.'

Jerry pushes his way past Darryl and he hears him crashing around the kitchen. Rather than follow, Darryl leans against the door frame. Again, he is reminded of Vivien in that scene. However Vivien in that scene produced a large gun and shot the would-be looter/rapist. Darryl wonders what he could do if he could lay hands on a gun. Since he can't, he realises he needs to don street clothes and venture back into the night. Surely someone he knows will put him up, at least temporarily, until he can convince his work that they can pay his salary direct to him again, and not the various online creditors.

Not having time to sort out his make-up Darryl redons his men's street disguise and heads off. For a boy/girl in distress there are a number of Soho watering holes where a saviour may be found. Unfortunately, Darryl knows that he lucked out with Jerry, for whom he was unknown and seemingly trustworthy, since no one who has been taken in by him before is likely to again invite him into their homes where he can take advantage of their charity. He doesn't even consider his oldest and dearest friends, aware that some of them have formed a club where they meet to swap horror stories of Darryl's invasion of their lives. He needs someone new to Soho, but already sufficiently set up to have a room for Darryl. He needs someone who doesn't demand a deposit upfront and who also fits with his/her idiosyncratic personal lifestyle. He looks in vain for Dolly. Dolly was an airline steward – as in Trolly Dolly – with whom he shared for six blissful months until he slept with Dolly's boyfriend and also inadvertently set fire to her flat. Dolly, though, has a short memory and a kind heart.

Helping himself to a free glass of water from the bar in Couscous, he peers through the gloom. Dolly has a thing for the young and if she was in town this is where she would hang out. But, knowing that this particular bar usually draws a crowd too young and insolvent to fulfil Darryl's present desperate need, he peers without much hope.

Although his expert eye fixes on some well-dressed young men and women, Darryl knows that they are probably still at home and their parents would be unlikely to look kindly on Darryl. Oh, he observes to himself, it's all too much to cope with. I could take a good hard look at myself but if I did that I'd have enough anguish to last for years and frankly I need all my energy for the present task. So I'll push regret to the back and sail forth carefree and composed and the solution to this present problem will fall into place.

At that moment the solution to Darryl's present problem is standing in the gloomiest part of Couscous, his pants around his ankles, while he models for a group of intimate friends his new metal groin arrangement. Most of Zac's peer group are, like him, twink types living on the get-high-now-pay-later edge. Only his best friend, Philip, holds down a 'respectable' job and takes home a salary he spends like ordinary people.

Since the bruising in Zac's privates has died down he has been itching to show off his metal arrangement. Yet the depths of Coucous are so gloomy that if it wasn't for the shards bouncing off the glitterball and catching the silver metal Darryl wouldn't even have known he was there. Catching the reflection, Darryl's heart gives a happy cry and he pushes his way through the punters standing round drinking and trading stories.

'Zac!' Darryl cries out. Noise from the crowd and the speakers drowns out his cry but it's not really necessary. He ingratiates himself between two young men who are asking Zac if it hurts and if they can try it on. For a moment the newcomer startles Zac but then he recognizes Darryl.

'Hi' he says and pulls up his shorts and pants.

'Don't mind me!' shouts Darryl.

'Yeah, sure' says Zac, buttoning and buckling. His two friends are disappointed. They both stand with hands outstretched ready to receive the metal wonder. Zac pushes his way past them and taking Darryl's arm leads him into the centre of the bar.

'How's Jerry?' shouts Zac.

'Oh' says Darryl, conscious of the need to present the situation in its best light.

'Oh he's dead.'

'What!' shrieks Zac.

'Yes, didn't you read about the … uh… Tsunami in Gran Canaria?'

'What???!' shrieks Zac.

'Yes, and his parents have suddenly appeared to take the flat. Apparently, he left it to them in his will.'

Zac grabs Darryl again and pulls him out of Couscous, onto the pavement. Darryl is aware of the cooling breeze now that sweaty bodies no longer surround him. He loves the night air yet he can't enjoy the sensual touch of it on his skin, since he has to keep thinking furiously hard.

'Yes, and it turns out they're big bigots. They came in and I was wearing a very simple set of pyjamas and fluffy shoes and they've thrown me out.'

Zac regards Darryl, his look of anguish replaced by one of anger.

'They can't do that. You've got a tenancy agreement. Haven't you?' The last in response to Darryl's helpless shoulder shake.

'Fine. I'll sort them anyway.' To Darryl's horror Zac begins storming off in the direction of the flat.

Think man/woman, think!

Darryl cries out and when Zac turns round he sees Darryl has fainted. He hurries over and drags him back into a vertical position.

'I can't. I just can't. I can't face those people. Knowing that Jerry has gone!'

Zac's face is still surprisingly grim for such a total twink.

'You don't worry, darling. I'll fight your battles.'

Darryl holds Zac's arm in a vice-like grip. 'No, don't leave me.' Then as though being struck by a new thought, he asks in a lighter tone 'You live around here, don't you?'

A few minutes later Darryl is scoping out Zac's plush studio apartment. Darryl sighs, considering that if Zac can afford such luxury on the money he brings in, exactly how much has he spent over the years on online gambling?

'This is wonderful!' cries Darryl.

Zac shrugs. 'It's only a poxy studio.'

'No, it's Angela-awesome. So clean and airy.'

'Look, you can only stay here temporarily. Just until I can get you some sort of compensation from Jerry's parents.'

'Oh don't bother about them!'

'No, it's only proper. Anyway, when I've got a client you'll have to be out somewhere.'

'Don't forget I've got a day job!'

'Yeah, I meant in the evening. I mean sometimes I get punters ringing on my bell at one or two in the morning. I charge them double.'

'So I'll have to get up and out anytime of the night?' asks Darryl dubiously.

'Yeah. There's always an all-night café open. I'll text you when it's safe to return.'

Darryl considers. He knows that once he's in bed and asleep nothing, but nothing and that includes anonymous, randy, visitors, is going to get him up again. However, as with all of his previous homes, the big trick is to get the key to the front door. Once he's in there's loads of leeway. He might even persuade Zac to let him sleep in the bathroom, or behind the kitchenette counter. Or to watch. It's happened before.

So he adopts his biggest shit-eating grin and nods enthusiastically. 'I can do that no problems.'

'And no men.'

Darryl sighs. Might as well turn his present dry run into a formal agreement. 'Also not a problem.'

Zac smiles, fishes in a drawer and proffers a key. Darryl's hand shoots out and he has to be careful not to show just how relieved he is to again have a resting place, even though Zac repeatedly reminds him the arrangement will be only temporary. With an inner smile to himself Darryl mentally recalls how many times someone has said that to him in the past. And how many times he stretched the word temporary as far as the next room before it, and the homeowner, snapped.

Insisting that he couldn't bear to see Zac fighting with Jerry's imaginary parents, Darryl scoots back to Jerry's home. There he scoops his possessions into bin bags and using Jerry's charge code, which he has previously memorised for the right occasion, calls for an Uber with plenty of baggage room.

He is on the pavement outside and just loading the last of the bags into the taxi when Jerry, obviously both drunk and high, staggers into view.

Darryl is too well bred, and fond of a big scene, to let the moment go unmarked. He has recently reread Arthur Hailey's 1960's blockbuster 'Hotel'. In it a luscious and sweet Marilyn Monroe type is forced to say goodbye to her hugely wealthy tycoon boyfriend, Curtis, because he's tired of her. Subsequently she gets into the fatal lift that plunges to the basement. She's not killed, however, and the tycoon realises, as her smashed body is taken to hospital, that he is actually madly in love with her. He begs the paramedics to treat her well and tells them as soon as she regains consciousness they will be married. This part Darryl has read many times over and it always makes him sob brokenly. Now, firmly in Marilyn character despite being in his work clothes, he walks over to Jerry and says in a tragic, breathless voice 'Goodbye dearest Curtie. I'll never forget you.'

Jerry is basically on another planet yet even to him something about this doesn't seem right and he blinks quizzically.

'I mean goodbye dearest Jerry' says Darryl. 'I'll never forget all your kindness.'

'Piss off, you giant sponge' mutters Jerry, his mind awash with chemicals that are staining the night before him into a myriad of shifting rainbow colours. 'And give me your key.'

Darryl takes his key to the flat out of his pocket and as Jerry reaches out for it Darry drops the key into the street where it makes a happy chinking sound and bounces merrily through a hole in the pavement. Leaving Jerry swearing, Darryl jumps into the taxi, which makes its way slowly through the streets towards Darryl's new home.

Eight. ALEC

Thanks to a cancellation I've been able to book a last-minute place at a very special retreat. Blythe Hall. It seems unbelievable to me yet there exists in the English countryside an estate to which homosexual men flock in order to spend a week being, well, gay. I found it while I was browsing for something less exalted, yet what could be better for exploring who I am, in the most congenial surroundings, I can't imagine.

I missed my previous session with Guy so I'm making up for it by being a few minutes early to this one. I ring and he opens. He's wearing a tiny, tight, low-cut shirt which I believe is some description of gym attire, plus little cotton shorts and as I glance up to down I can't help admiring the mid-section bulge.

'Alec!' he says, clearly flustered. 'I didn't know you were coming. You didn't confirm another appointment.'

'I think I did' I say suavely, retrieving my mobile and checking my texts. To discover that I didn't actually send the text. 'Oh, so sorry. I'll make myself scarce.'

'No, that's fine, come in.'

I follow Guy into his home. The area in the open-plan sitting room is tidy enough for our purposes so I sit down without being asked. Guy is still flustered and says he's going to change. He walks out the room sending a text, presumably to the person he had been expecting. I look around and see on the coffee table between us a large tube of what I believe is called KY jelly lubricant. I lean forward and push the tube around but don't know what else to do so I check my work messages. Guy returns, having changed into a track suit which in my opinion is not quite sufficient for therapy work. Presumably it was quickest. He bears two glasses of water, and I sip one.

'So sorry about the confusion' he says.

'I take it you were expecting someone else?'

Guy is silent for a moment as though determining whether or not to share this tiny part of his personal life with me. To help, I point my finger at the tube of KY.

Guy leaps up, snatches the tube and hides it in a drawer. He turns to me, smiles ruefully and sits down again.

'Well, since my private life keeps intruding, I can tell you that … I'm making changes. My partner is most probably moving out. When I opened the door I was expecting someone I've been messaging on Grindr.'

'Thank you, Guy. I'm touched you feel able to be open about yourself. You know, on my side I go through agonies wondering how much I can bear to disclose. Seeing you as a real person is very helpful.'

Guy nods in agreement. 'Yes, I've found that. Don't want to do it too much though.'

We sit in silence.

'I suppose I should update you. I know I said previously that I did not believe I was homosexual. I would now like to reverse that statement.'

For the rest of the session I talk out some of my confusion and grief. Guy is a sympathetic listener. I tell him about my planned visit to Blythe Hall. A shadow crosses his face.

'You have an opinion?' I ask.

Guy thinks before replying. 'No, I don't think so. I'll be interested to hear what you find there.'

‘With so many men …’ I begin but I can’t continue. Guy also seems to be reluctant to say too much in advance, which I find a little discouraging. I would have welcomed more enthusiasm from him.

The taxi from the station knows all about Blythe Hall. I have the feeling the house is both famous and notorious in the area. I am not bothered: in fact I rather wish to wrap myself in its reputation. I step out onto a gravel circle which connects the house with the drive. It makes a satisfying crunching sound under my shoes. I have brought only an overnight bag, so I don’t require a porter. I take a breath to gather my bearings. The house is huge, the wide Arts and Crafts portico with stained glass double doors welcoming. Yet it’s the fauna who particularly impress. Everywhere there are men, mainly young, talking quietly and walking, criss-crossing the driveway and the grass and fields beyond. I shudder with excitement.

Inside I explain who I am and I’m told the cancellation is for a single room, which pleases me greatly. In my room I unpack my modest bag and open the curtain. It faces a blank wall and from the aromatic smells that infuse the room I take it I am above the kitchen. I sigh. Well, I wanted to be here. Perhaps next time I’ll have better luck with the accommodation. In the corridor I can hear quick footsteps and excited voices calling to each other. I sit on the bed for a moment. It’s happened so quickly, I can’t believe I have landed in what I am disposed to think of as the Mecca of homosexual life.

I wonder if I should change but I think not. So I go out as I am, in formal casual dress of trousers and a striped shirt. I wondered about dress code but all the brochure had to say is that nudity is not permitted in the public rooms. Which only leads me to wonder where it *is* permitted.

As I shuffle into the corridor a group of four young men run by me. For a moment I am caught up in a torrent of warm flesh, bright colours, youthful exuberance. It's as wonderful as I could ever have dreamed of.

'Come on!' one of them cries and I indicate myself. Are they inviting me to join them?

'We'll lose our place' cries another and they continue on their way, one of them stripping off his shirt to loud laughter. At the end of the corridor they disappear into a particular room and slam the door. I stand outside the closed door. On it is a ceramic tile emblazoned 'Bathroom'. Inside I can hear excited splashing. It would appear the four are taking a communal bath. In this moment I believe I would give half my kingdom, or at least my house, to have the courage to push the door open and join them. Instead I stand rooted, appalled both by the deep desire flooding my chest and a prickly sweat that has broken out on my forehead at the possible consequences of such a reckless action. For a minute I stand and listen to splashes and snatched sentences then a couple of smartly dressed men in their 30s appear at the other end of the corridor and I shuffle off and down the staircase.

Downstairs there is a communal room with a refreshment table at one end. About 30 men aged between 20 and 60 are sitting or standing around. Some hold a hot drink, some a cold can. A couple on the upper end of the age scale are tucking into sandwiches and pieces of cake or biscuits. I check my wrist because I believe dinner hour is coming up soon and am again disappointed to remember that Jerry has never returned my watch.

'Hello. You must be new' says a cheerful voice. I turn and see it is coming from a man approximately 30.

'Yes. I've never seen anything like this.'

'Oh, I only meant I hadn't seen you at Blythe before. I'm Richard, I'm your weekend rep.'

'So delighted to meet you' I say, holding out my hand. He declines to shake it.

'You just enjoy yourself' he says, allowing a young man who has just appeared in the doorway to catch his eye. In a moment Richard is by his side.

'Hello. You must be new' I hear him say. The youth recoils slightly. I can't help staring. The newcomer is slight of figure, with wide innocent eyes and a generous mouth. His hair is thick and brushed back over a middle parting. He wears proper trousers, a shirt and in deference to the slight chill, an expensive cashmere jumper.

'I'm Richard. You're welcome to stay by my side all weekend. I know it's difficult to make friends at first.'

Well, honestly. Richard is clearly using his position to gain an unfair advantage over the rest of us. I should walk over and introduce myself.

'I'm Archie. I've never been in a place like this before.'

'Oh' says Richard, his voice becoming even more oily, 'You can lean on me.'

Oh really? I think. I've never been in a place like this either, but you couldn't be bothered to help me. Of course, there is no possible way in which I could introduce myself to the vision called Archie, so I make myself a cup of tea. I'm lingering round the urn in the hope that someone will join me and we can get into spontaneous conversation but looking around it's almost as if the rest of them are giving the urn a wide berth. My mouth automatically clenches. Oh my Lord. It's me. They're avoiding me.

I seek out the two oldest men in the room. There can't be more than a few years between us. I walk over to them before they can leave and introduce myself. With growing cynicism I observe their attempting to choose between a sudden engagement out of doors and their natural politeness. Conversation is strained until I give them my surname.

'Oh. Are you anything to do with Bland & Co?'

'I'm the Chairman and Managing Director.'

This apparently makes a difference. It turns out the younger, Roger, has been trying to speak to someone at Bland for a while. I watch, again cynically, as his companion, Peter, understands that this is turning into an unexpected work-related networking event and that I must be charmed. I finish by giving them both my card and, saddened by how the outside world has invaded my personal heaven, I walk out the French glass doors and onto the spacious patio.

Here men are enjoying the evening. Men who have come together are talking quietly. Men who have only just met are making hilarious points and laughing loudly. Men who are alone and apparently on the prowl are sizing up possible opportunities. I flatter myself I am able to look at all this and not be taken in.

'Hello. Haven't seen you before.' I hear a friendly voice and turn round but it's not being addressed to me. I smile in any case and move on. I decide to walk as far as I can before the terrain becomes inadvisable for town shoes. Ten minutes later I return to where there are still groups of men talking among themselves.

There doesn't seem to be much going on in the way of organisation. Is this all I can expect?

It's pleasant enough although I'm starting to feel over-exposed and I wish someone would talk to me. I'm beginning to feel the old, familiar feeling of shame, starting in my feet and working its way up. I think of my bedroom, facing the blank wall. I realise that most of the other rooms are shared, and that would have been preferable. Sharing means I would at least have one man to talk to. As it's unfolding the only person who wants to talk to me is interested in my work self, which I have come here to very definitely forget.

Richard appears through the double glass doors like the second lead in a drawing room comedy. 'Ladies and gentlemen, boys and girls. Time for opening address in the Wilde Room.' I notice the new young man, Archie, is still hanging around Richard.

The Wilde Room is large enough to host a ball and was presumably the ballroom when the house was in private hands. There is a disparate group of chairs and other seating available, ranging from a few comfortable armchairs through a number of soulless plastic chairs to what looks like beanbags and futons. The beanbags and futons are surprisingly popular and young men, exclusively, are sprawled over them, talking furiously. I note two men about 30 are passionately embracing, even fumbling inside each other's clothes, while around them the rest of the throng is entirely unaware, or more likely, not bothered. I sink with a grunt into the most comfortable armchair. I watch how the others signal their belief in who they are by how they select a chair. Since most of the chairs are the soulless plastic kind does it follow that if you sit in one you are basically unimaginative and mediocre? Does sprawling on the floor on a futon signify a wanton attitude? Or just that it's fun? In fact, I now regret my choice because on either side two men almost as old as me have taken the other armchairs. Like three solemn judges we watch while the younger men toss themselves around with great abandon or talk passionately and intimately to each other.

In the midst of the throng and the din I am suddenly moved as I have never been previously. All this life. It's always been like this. It could always have been like this for me. So sad that it's always passed me by. And I am so, so late coming to the fair.

I am aware that tears are coursing down my cheeks. One of other armchair occupants turns to me, holding out his hankie.

‘Your first?’ he enquires. ‘I was a wreck the whole of the first time. Now I live for these weekends.’

I wipe my eyes. ‘Thank you so much. I will wash and return it tomorrow.’

‘No hurry. I always bring a dozen.’

‘My name’s Alec Bland.’

‘Miles Pullman. And this fossil is John’ he says, indicating the occupant of the other armchair.

‘I was thinking we looked like three solemn judges’ I say, pleased that my voice is no longer wavering.

‘I was thinking I could take off all my clothes, cover myself with baby oil, and throw myself into the throng’ says Miles. ‘Except they frown on lewd exhibitions in the public areas. In the private areas, of course, they enthusiastically encourage it.’

‘I’m being joined by my husband’ reports John. ‘Thank God.’

I think this a little harsh until I think about what is at stake this weekend. Although the brochure promises a weekend of activities and interesting talks it’s becoming clear that the principal attraction of Blythe Hall is who you can meet, and how many. Which fills me with hope as well as dread. I’ve now read enough online to know that there are some men who are specifically attracted to much older men. I fit that bill, yet how do I go about making myself available? What if they take my formal demeanour to indicate a lack of interest? Frankly, if there are signals, do I believe myself competent to intercept and take advantage of them?

Richard, with Archie in puppylike tow, appears and rings a bell. He introduces Andrew, who it turns out runs Blythe Hall. Andrew is in his late 40s and from the over-loud laughter with which Miles on my right greets all his half-witticisms I gather that Miles finds him attractive. There are 65 of us. We all have to stand in a long line and count off either one, two or three. I'm a three. For the whole weekend whenever we split into smaller groups I will be with the threes. We do in fact split shortly afterwards and the threes move to the Crisp Room. Smaller, with more beanbags and only one armchair. I resolve not to take it, and instead sink down warily on one of the beanbags. I can feel my back cracking as it connects with cotton cover and polystyrene balls.

The first session is quite pleasant. Our workshop leader is called Alex. He's in his early 30s and most of the men seem to know him. In what context they know him is not made specific although I suspect group baths are common. One of the men talks about his breakup with his boyfriend. Another talks about his flatmate's unfortunate habits. A third talks about the man at work with whom he is manically besotted. All in all, just people talking about the everyday. Made, for me, entirely extraordinary by the circumstances, the gender, and the easy acceptance of everyone in the room. When we break for dinner I shift in my beanbag. I honestly can't work out how one becomes vertical from the damned thing. Everyone else has left and I'm still trying to get up. Alex stands patiently waiting at the door, ready to turn off the light.

'Are you having a rest, Alec?' he asks politely.

'If you must – I can't get out of this bloody bean bag.'

A smile creases Alex's firm lips which he instantly discards. He comes over to me and pulls one of my arms. Instantly a flash of pain rockets from my shoulder down my back and I cry out.

'Ah' he says. 'Wait and I'll get some help.'

A minute later there are four of them trying to get me up. They talk about me as though I'm not there.

'What if we turn him over?'

'And then he can't breathe?'

'What if we get some sort of lever? You know, 'give me a long enough lever and I'll move the world.'

'We don't have any levers. There's four of us. He's not *that* heavy.'

'It's more like we can't get a proper grip.'

'Or if we do, he howls. I don't want to think we're hurting him.'

'Should I call Richard?

'No!' I say. I don't know why but I don't want Richard and his smooth professional attitude seeing me in this humiliating situation.

'We could grease him up?' says one of the men dubiously.

'No' says Alex. 'Charlie, me and you will stand behind him and pull him up. Ryan, you wedge yourself under his feet so he can't slip. He'll only be able to go up.'

I dread how my back is going to respond to this treatment but I have no say. Alex and Charlie stand behind me and I can feel their strong arms wrapping round my shoulders and upper arms. Ryan I can feel wedging his feet against mine. Then Alex gives the signal and miraculously I am lifted up. My feet scramble and I manage to stabilise myself. I wipe my brow, because I am sweating, and stammer genuine thanks to the four men. They shrug it off and move out the room. They are giving me a moment by myself. I use it to feel humiliation worse than I have ever experienced. All the way back to my room I am determined to pack and flee.

Yet when I walk along my corridor, hearing noise through the closed doors or catching a glimpse of someone reading, changing or chatting, I acknowledge that leaving this wonderful environment even a second before I have to would be a tremendous waste. So what if they are having a laugh about the old walrus they had to rescue? Do they think they will never get older? And, as I'm changing for dinner, I also realise that everything at Blythe revolves around acceptance of who we are. Why *would* they laugh at me?

As I walk down to dinner I think about my father. I wonder if the dead can look down on the living, and if right now he is spinning in his grave? If so, I hope he has an excellent view of his son, as he prepares to join all the other men looking forward to a shared dinner on this wholly remarkable weekend.

Nine. DENNIS

That Friday just gone, Dennis checks his appointment calendar and discovers with a twinge of annoyance that his PA, Philip, on receiving the news that Dennis's meeting with Sandra is confidential, has entered it as 'Secret Meeting.' Dennis corrects this, mindful that the dirtier the business, the fewer people you want involved until the matter is ready to blow up. Sandra appears a little late and by this time Dennis is so irritated that he keeps her waiting while, he says curtly, he reads a document so timeous that it must be perused without any delay.

Sandra occupies herself staring at Dennis's fingernails. She marvels over their polished perfection. She used to think he wore men's nail polish but lately she's been leaning towards the idea that Dennis naturally has nails like the inside of an oyster. They gleam with a superb inner lustre that puts gold to shame.

After a few minutes Dennis feels reconciled by Sandra's deferential manner so he folds away the paper and rewards Sandra's patience with a conspirator's smile.

'So the ancient nuisance has already left for the weekend. He's slipping.'

'Yes. He told Rochelle he was off to visit his late wife's sister again. But.'

'But?'

'It's only that last Monday I asked him how he'd enjoyed the weekend and he didn't answer. His expression … his expression …'

'Was that of a walrus whose weekend plans went badly awry?'

The two exchange a brief cackle.

'Exactly. So I can't compute that he would do the whole thing again so soon.'

'Hmm' says Dennis, using one immaculately chiselled fingernail to flip open his leather-bound desk notebook. 'I'll make a note. Might try to catch him out next week.'

'Of course, we are in agreement that we're only doing this for the company.'

Dennis stares at Sandra, then sees where she's heading and nods seriously. Under the surface both of them know they are conspiring against Alec wholly to advance their own careers at the expense of his happiness. Yet they might end up in court at some point and it helps to be able to recall conversations like this one, even though both are aware of the lie.

'We have noticed a sharp decline in his intellectual powers, following the death of his wife.'

'The tragic death of his dear wife' amends Sandra.

'The tragic and regrettable death of his wife Alison, the centre of his life and, if I may add, a woman I always thought of as the heart of the company' says Dennis, unwilling to let Sandra score points in any sphere.

'Yes' says Sandra, 'so what we do we do with heavy hearts.'

'Heavy hearts that have laboured long into the night to arrive at any other solution to our highly concerning situation. Yet having found none, it is with deep personal pain that we arrive at the steps which we must take' says Dennis.

'That's good, although I'd say 'crucial' rather than 'highly concerning'' says Sandra thoughtfully.

Dennis looks up from his luxury notepad and fixes his eyes on Sandra.

‘We agreed we would work together on this?’

‘Yes. So?’

‘Stop pissing about on trivialities.’

Sandra takes in her breath with a hiss. If she were a man he would not treat her like this. Then again, she considers, if she were a man she wouldn’t be wearing a dress or make-up, or be called Sandra. Nevertheless, she is beginning to resent Dennis’s assumption that as the man he naturally has prime position and she is somewhere to the side. This isn’t the time to have it out with Dennis, though. That must wait until the main issue has been successfully concluded.

‘What have we got on him so far?’ asks Dennis, licking his moist lips slightly and discreetly rubbing the fingers of his immaculate hands.

‘Well’ says Sandra. ‘With regards to his behaviour towards poor Jenny…’

‘Don’t egg it’ says Dennis.

‘With regards to his behaviour towards Jenny in reception …’

‘I know where Jenny works’ snaps Dennis. Sandra expels a grunt of irritation and Dennis coughs to indicate he is remorseful.

‘Re Jenny we can definitely get him on multiple counts of sexism. Those things he said to her were deeply shocking. There are a number of women in the building who are now terrified of him approaching them.’

‘Yes, that’s good. Are you going to be one of the terrified women?’

‘Me?!’ says Sandra. ‘The old goat must try. He’ll get my umbrella wedged up his flabby arse.’

'We'll say that you've been deeply perturbed by these events and you know it's having an effect on office morale' decides Dennis.

Sandra nods. 'And then there's the remark he made to the temp. Alex. We can get him on xenophobia, and since Alex is biracial, we can probably get him on racism as well.'

Dennis stretches and yawns. 'Yes, all good so far.' There is a buzz from his mobile, to which he devotes a quick glance. What he sees causes him to sit up and he gathers the mobile close to him, as though, thinks Sandra, to avoid her reading its contents.

'But we need something bigger, something that smashes any defence he can produce. For example, he could blame it on momentary lapses brought on by his present loss.'

'Grievous loss' Sandra prefers.

'I don't give a shit what sort of loss it is' says Dennis. 'The point is we need something bigger. Something he's doing all the time. Not just a momentary lapse but something that's worked into the fabric of his day.'

Sandra flicks through everything she has on her boss and shakes her head. 'He's so vanilla. There's nothing like that I can think of.'

'We've got three months before the next meeting of the Board and Principal Shareholders. He's started well enough, I'm sure it's only a matter of waiting and watching.'

'We'll be terribly, terribly sad to lose Alec. His helmsmanship has been a constant support and inspiration to us all' ventures Sandra.

'But we think it's best for the old nuisance if you become M.D. and I become Chair' says Dennis.

'Quite. And once we've cleaned up that sentiment, removing a remark that could be termed ageist, we're good to go before the Board.'

At the word 'clean', although Sandra does not understand why, Dennis's eyes widen with a strange gleaming. Sandra has only seen eyes behave like that once before, and that was when a man she didn't know stopped his car and asked her if she would like a lift to the sweetshop. She had been five at the time and had run screaming back into the safety of the school playground. Quitting Dennis's office and heading back to her own she stands for a moment in silence, making a mental comparison with the hateful memory, and Dennis a couple of minutes ago. She shakes her head and files it away, perhaps at some point it will reveal its meaning.

Sitting at the desk allotted to Dennis's PA, Rochelle has been finishing up for the day. She sees Sandra apparently lost in reverie and asks 'Did you want anything, Sandra?' Sandra comes back to reality with a little jolt. She looks down at Rochelle, noticing for the first time that Rochelle has very acceptable eyes. She's also done something becoming with her hair. It is the talk of the office how Rochelle has apparently burned her surgical stockings along with her bra. For the first time Sandra can compliment her on her appearance.'

'You look festive, Rochelle' she says. 'Going somewhere special?'

Rochelle, busy with last minute filing, looks up at her in mild surprise. 'Why does everyone keep asking if I'm doing something special? It's same old same old for Rochelle from here till the grave.'

Sandra silently reflects that Rochelle's social world has yet to catch up with her external changes.

'That's a bit miz' says Sandra kindly. 'We should go out sometime and talk about it.'

Sandra is not prepared for the huge wattage smile Rochelle sends her way in reply. It causes Sandra's heart to flip slightly in its bony cage.

‘That would be really, really wonderful’ says Rochelle in a new, soft tone. A little taken back by the warmth of Rochelle’s response, Sandra nods with a smile and returns to her own office. She makes a mental note that it really doesn’t take much to make someone’s day. She also makes a note to think about why it’s taken her until now in her life to realise that. Then she makes a last note that she needn’t actually think about that, since all her energy is required for higher tasks. She wants to savour Dennis’s acknowledgment that she will be MD.

Left in his office, Dennis closes the door and returns the last call to his mobile.

‘Hello, you called me a few minutes ago.’

‘Hi. Is someone there? Speak up?’

‘I can’t. I’m in the office. Can you hear me …’ Dennis pushes his chair back and leans painfully under his desk. ‘Can you hear me now?’

‘Uh … okay. I sort of. So why you calling?’

‘I’m answering your ad.’

‘Yeah that figures.’

‘Did you mean everything in it?’

‘You pay per word so I’d be pretty dense to put in words I didn’t mean’ is the gracious reply.

‘Very well’ says Dennis hastily, aware that these things are delicate and he doesn’t want to come across as a crank call. ‘I have a vacancy this evening, in fact. How are you fixed?’

‘Depends on how long you want.’

‘I’ll need a couple of hours’ says Dennis, suddenly reducing his voice to a hoarse whisper as he hears voices in the corridor outside.

'Fine. Cost you three hundred.' Dennis is aware that the voice imparts this figure with a certain ambivalence. Yet he's not about to start a price war on the phone. 'That's fine. I'll bring cash.'

'I'll text you the address' says the voice and then rings off. Dennis stares into space, his heart racing, his limbs unable to move for the intense excitement. A minute later he receives a text with an address in Soho. This is the cue for lightning movement as he locks away anything in any shape or form confidential. The innocent man sleeps with an unlocked door, and Dennis sleeps with numerous door locks and a kitchen knife under his pillow. Those who deal in treachery and violence usually expect it in return.

It would be stating the obvious to note that the building is sordid and the inhabitants some of Soho's lowest dregs. Dennis wouldn't have it any other way. Traversing the corridor Dennis can hear from behind closed doors and curtained windows the expected sounds of Soho at dusk. Music from the ghetto. Crying babies, no doubt the inevitable results of their mothers' easy virtue. The odd argument and one set of powerful smacks. Dennis comes to a halt, rings the bell and licks his already moist lips in thrilled anticipation of the pleasures of the next couple of hours.

Jerry opens the door. A couple of weeks returned from Gran Canaria he is starting to lose the tan which leant a becoming flush to his sallow cheeks.

Dennis quickly hurries past Jerry and into the flat. As he goes by Jerry Dennis takes in a deep lungful and he's disappointed.

'What?' mutters Jerry. He's not used to adverse punter feedback.

'I had hoped … your ad did … Oh well, I suppose you'll do' says Dennis, conscious that he could put more enthusiasm into it.

'Listen I haven't had a bath or a wash for nearly two weeks'! thunders Jerry.

'Yes, no doubt you're telling the truth. I suppose I … you do advertise as The Human Pig.'

'Actually' says Jerry, made sarcastic by the lack of appreciation from his latest punter, 'pigs are exceptionally clean-living animals. I don't know why they get such a shitty press.'

Something in Jerry's response raises a question for Dennis.

'You're more articulate than I was expecting, too. Did you go to Uni?'

'Are you here to offer me a job or what?' snarls Jerry. 'You're on the clock you know.'

This answer is sufficiently aggressive to reassure Dennis that The Pig Man, although disappointing in odour, is still unpleasant enough generally to make for a thoroughly satisfying encounter.

'And if you want to see my sty' Jerry continues and strides to the closed kitchen door. Dennis follows him and gasps. Jerry's kitchen is a masterwork of strewn pizza boxes, empty bottles, discarded newspapers, dirty plates, pots, cups and glasses, and general offensiveness. Over everything hangs a pall of neglect so palpable Dennis believes he can part it with his hands. It goes without saying that the floor is sticky to the shoe.

'This is … well' says Dennis, looking at Jerry with admiration.

'Tell me Pig Man don't know his territory' mutters Jerry.

'Oh, please don't be upset with me' says Dennis, pulling something shiny and plastic from his back pockets.

'You get on your hands and knees and scrub' Jerry responds.

'Oh, I will, sir, I will.'

Covering his exquisite fingers with the shiny plastic gloves, Dennis removes from his briefcase a square of black vinyl. He carefully places this on the floor, then knees. Jerry stands over him.

'Scrub this floor!' he commands.

'But master, I don't have any soapy water!' cries Dennis.

Jerry grabs him by the hair, pulling his head back, causing his mouth to drop open.

'Use your spit man!'

Two hours, observes Dennis two hours later, just flies by. He's only completed a scrub of half the kitchen floor by the time Dennis signals his time is up by kicking him in the rear. Dennis obediently stands up, neatly folds away his square and gloves, and reaches for his wallet.

'That was fun' says Jerry. 'You're good at this.'

Dennis usually likes his master to stay in character, even for the payoff and final goodbyes. But tonight, with nothing more to look forward to the entire weekend, Dennis is in a mood to share.

'I need this down time' he replies.

'Bit shit at work?' asks Jerry sympathetically.

'You don't know the half. Big plans to get rid of the MD and Chairman – one person – and divide his role into two. I'll be the Chairman' Dennis explains.

'Yeah?' asks Jerry. Like many people who live on the breadline, he is fascinated by those who actually contribute to the running of the economy.

‘And it’s harder because the woman I’m doing it with is a complete bitch. Completely untrustworthy, of course.’

‘Couldn’t you find someone more trustworthy?’ asks Jerry with genuine concern.

‘The trouble is, I’ve tried. For some reason nobody trusts me’ says Dennis with honesty.

‘I like you’ says Jerry with emphasis on the ‘I’.

Dennis regards Jerry with genuine affection. This is what he loves about his fetish. Every so often you encounter someone who is genuinely kind and loving. People on the outside don’t understand that S & M fetishists have exactly the same needs as others, they just go about getting theirs differently.

‘You’re a kind soul’ says Dennis.

‘And you owe me three hundred’ says Jerry. Chastised for his over-familiarity, Dennis hastily counts out the sum into Jerry’s ready hand.

‘Ta mate.’

‘I hope this is only the first time’ says Dennis. ‘I’ve still got the other half of your kitchen floor. And that doesn’t even get us started on the washing up! Plus your kitchen table is at least another half session.’

‘That’s not all’ says Jerry, opening the bathroom door. At the sight of Jerry’s bathroom, a space that would be not only condemned but permanently sealed by Council edict, Dennis clutches his middle region as his sexual organs, having been under maximum stimulation over the last two hours, finally explode.

Jerry knows exactly what to do now, if he wants to be certain Dennis will return. Dragging Dennis by the ear he thrusts him out the flat and slams the door. In the corridor Dennis utters a last happy sigh of fulfilment and then makes his way back to the street, clutching his briefcase in front of him.

In a taxi, returning to his apartment which is always scrubbed so thoroughly that brain surgery could be performed, he flips happily between memories of the past two hours, and his anticipation of the fulfilment of his career ambitions. 'Dennis Pitt, Chairman' he says aloud, 'has such a nice ring to it. And I deserve it. I work so hard. I've sacrificed everything else in a man's life for career. I've done the figures. It all adds up.'

And to top it off there's always the chance that the old nuisance will have a heart attack or a stroke or something timely. Although in a way that would be a disappointment, since Dennis's loins are girded up and weaponised for a hostile takeover.

Ten. ALEC

Alec opens his tired yet happy eyes to discover the sun is already up and shining while he is still wallowing in his single room at Blythe. During the night he was disturbed by a series of indistinct yet loud thumps from the corridor, accompanied by stifled giggles, that he interpreted fondly as one set of young men playfully attacking another. After using the on-suite shower, another ostensible asset that, he realises too late, merely keeps him from the imagined joys of group showering, he dresses appropriately. A perusal of the events brochure seems to offer an event where, if Alec has interpreted correctly, the participants get naked and then compliment each other on their nude bodies. Although the idea of being in a room full of naked, chatty, men is deeply appealing, Alec is paralysed by a concern that he hasn't read the brochure properly. What if no one can think of anything positive to say, and instead comment negatively on his unadorned appearance?

Perhaps, he thinks, someone else will have previously attended the workshop and can either reassure him or put him off entirely. Perhaps Miles or John from the previous evening? Throwing a pullover over his shoulders he quits his room and proceeds to the staircase.

Breakfast is served in the same large room as dinner. Polished oak floor, scrubbed wooden table tops, decent wooden chairs with an assortment of gaily coloured cushions. Posters on the wall are lively and seem to have been chosen for having some connection to gay men. These include Dirk Bogarde's breakthrough drama *Victim*, a couple of Joan Collins sexy comedies, *Maurice* and Antonioni's *Blow Up*. Alec is eager to enter into the fun of the new day and a little disappointed to observe there is only one other man in the room. The other looks as though he hasn't slept at all. As Alec watches the other man, slim, slight and somewhat dishevelled, grasps a huge glass bowl full of muesli and pours the bowl into his canvas rucksack. When the dishevelled one sees Alec cautiously approaching, he throws him a cheeky smile and raises a finger to his own lips in a universal gesture of 'don't say who did it.' Alec smiles, happy to participate in a gay deception.

'What's your name?' asks Alec.

Zac, for it is he, is on strict instructions from Darryl to work the buffet and replenish their parlous provisions cupboard. He is about to share his name with Alec when a group of four rowdy 20-and-30-year-olds barge in and their excited laughter rings through the room. Zac with his contraband rucksack quits the room while the four newcomers, ignoring Alec's cordial greeting, descend on the buffet like brightly attired gannets.

A few minutes later Alec is munching toast, marooned at the end of one of the tables while the other breakfast arrivals cluster at tables on the other side. Surely, he ponders, they aren't deliberately steering a path away from me? Surely it's merely that as each one arrives they see someone they already know? Alec believes he would like another cup of coffee so he returns to the refreshments table. There he spots Richard, the weekend rep, from the previous evening. Richard exchanges a few words with Alec before pushing past him and re-joining a young man. Alec watches gloomily as Richard literally seduces the young man with a combination of gentle pats to the arm, dazzling smiles, and words which send the young man into peals of delighted laughter. Alec sighs deeply, returns to his lonely seat which has taken on the feel of a desert island, and pretends to be engrossed in his brochure.

A minute later Alec hears a deep and resonant voice asking him if he is keeping the table for anyone. He lifts his eyes from the brochure hopefully and sees before him an elderly man, equipped with a walking stick, and with a plaster over his face which hides one of his eyes. The other eye, weak and milky, regards Alec dispassionately. In an instant

Alec enters fully into the rules of gay life. He realises that if he allows the newcomer to sit next to him that the newcomer will thereafter always seek him out at meals. He also understands that the young men around him are not being unkind to him personally, they are simply keeping to their own level of attractiveness. Just as they have discreetly cast Alec adrift, so Alec does not want to bring this undesirable new flotsam onto his desert island. Alec smiles regretfully.

'Sorry old man, I'm expecting a whole party.'

The man takes a moment to absorb this, then he nods and moves away, taking instead a seat at a table where there is a suitable gap between him and the younger men engaged in animated conversation. Alec sits and ponders deeply. He is shocked at his own behaviour and wishes he had the courage to invite the other older man back to eat with him. Yet he also knows this will merely underline to the entire room that the two will spend each meal together. Alec believes he has waited too long to feel a part of a room full of gay men, he has put up his whole life with obliging first his dreadful father and then his demanding wife, and he is damned if he will continue to be an aged Cinderella, taking her wretched place in the kitchen. Even if, he thinks, he has to eat all his meals on his own, he prefers that to being stuck with the empties. The fellow empties, he adds with a becoming honesty.

The meal over, the teeth cleaning, flossing and group showering accomplished, the whole group meets in the big room. Alec sees the one-eyed man who accosted him at breakfast has already found one of the three comfortable armchairs. He sees also that the man has kept one of the other armchairs for Alec. His first thought is to ignore this and join the younger men, then he remembers the beanbag farce of the previous evening. He also thinks that he can associate with the one-eyed man in the big room without this meaning they are a table for two at mealtime, so he shuffles over and greets the man with a polite smile.

'There you are' says the man, apparently unperturbed by Alec's rudeness at breakfast. 'I saved you a seat.'

'So I see' says Alec, throwing his bulk into the chair, which groans politely.

'My name's Donny. I used to be called Donald but changed my name after the wretched Trump business' he explains.

'Donny, hello, I'm Alec.'

'Isn't this a lovely room?'

Both men look around the room. The interior itself is nothing special. It's large, which is always in a room's favour, and painted a light green which is always a mistake. There are more gay-related posters, which makes the inclusion of a poster advertising the last Conservative Party conference a bit of a puzzle. Perhaps it was donated by Michael Portillo?

'Yes, very colourful' says Alec.

'I meant the men' responds Donny, with a complacent smirk.

'Yes, and like the beasts in the fields or the birds of the air, we can see but not touch.'

There is a moment, then Donny utters a deep and apparently highly amused grunt. He turns the last of Alec's remarks over in delight. 'See but not touch…' Donny laughs and repeats the phrase. Then he regards Alec from his one still working eye. 'I estimate I've had at least a dozen of the lads in this room.'

Alec emits a grunt in which disbelief and hope are equally mixed.

'Well, maybe not a *dozen* in *this* room' says Donny. 'But see that little lad there, with the rucksack? I've had him a couple of times, lovely little piece. And that one there with the yellow hair and red T-shirt?

And I dare say, if I worked my way through the rest of the room, I'd be able to add a few more to my list.'

Alec has the advantage over Donny in that he has two good eyes. He uses both to goggle at Donny, with his mouth dropped so low Donny has an excellent view of his dental work. Then reality intrudes.

'I suppose' he says, 'that you have to pay them a lot of money?'

With his one eye Donny's ability to communicate visually is impaired yet he is still able to respond to this with an almighty wink.

'You're not saying' says Alec, 'that you don't pay?'

'Oh' says Donny negligently, 'the odd dinner. Perhaps a bottle of aftershave at Christmas. It's against my religion to pay. I never have and I never will.'

'I'm sorry' says Alec. 'I just can't believe that.'

Donny regards Alec from his one working eye. 'Alec, I started having sex with men when I was 11. I began by working my way through the alphabet. So I had an Alan, a Bert, a Charles… When I got to the end – and I had to go to Israel to get a Ziggie – I began utilising the London post code. Beginning with N1 which was Islington. Now I'm up to Brixton which is SE24. There are so many beautiful men in SE24 I think I may choose to have my ashes strewn about its hallowed streets.'

Alec is conscious of the need for a stiff drink. One not being available he merely wipes his hand across his face.

'I'm so sorry. It's not that I don't believe you, Donny. It's just that …'

'You're new to this?' asks Donny.

Alec nods.

'Don't tell me. Never knew you were gay until something happened in the family, and now you're here making up for lost time?'

Alec nods.

'So, I'm guessing you stayed at home until your parents died then you moved in with a sister, and she's just passed on?'

'Worse! I was terrorised by my father and forced to marry. It's my wife who's just passed on.'

'But' askes Donny hopefully, 'you've always been able to get out for a bit on the side? Fumbles in the pub, wanks in the park, furtive intercourse in sordid railway hotels?'

'Never' says Alec. 'I'm a virgin.'

'Shut up! You're a virgin?' asks Donny in a voice both carrying and crystal clear. It is unfortunate that at the same time Andrew the workshop leader has raised his hand for group silence. The group is in the perfect place, at the perfect time, to receive the news. There is a moment's silence then a huge wave of giggle runs from one side of the room to the other. Alec wishes the ground would open and swallow him bodily. Acknowledging that that would take a considerable effort from nature, he wishes he had never come to wretched Blythe at all.

Andrew, however, is entirely unmoved.

'Welcome to one and all. Hope you slept well and when you weren't sleeping you were taking advantage of the lube and condom dispensers?' There is another giggle at this, with some furtive punching and tweaking of hair.

'So, you already know that after the break we'll be meeting in our ones, twos and threes? The weather's a bit crap so we'll be switching around activities. This morning ones will be drawing, twos will be preparing their presentation for the group talent show and threes will be having their naked encounter.'

A babble of excitement greets this announcement.

'Oh Lord' mutters Alec.

'What's the matter?' asks Donny.

'I'm a three' Alec explains.

'Oh that's not a problem. We can swap for the morning. I'm a one, so happy drawing. '

'But I'll still have to join in the naked embarrassment with the ones.'

'Absolutely not, we'll just swap back.'

'But doesn't that mean you'll have to endure two sessions of the naked encounter?'

'Two?' asks Donny with indignation. 'I'm renowned for my ability to muscle my way into all three!'

Alec sits back, the better to take in the full bulk of Donny, who is beaming with pure pleasure.

'But my good man – I mean, look at you!'

Donny knows exactly to what Alec is referring and it doesn't put him off.

'Since I was eleven' Donny explains. 'I've thought of myself as irresistible to other men. And as long as I never, never stray from that point of view, I've always found that other men are quite happy to take my word on it.'

Donny leads the charge out the room to the various entertainments. Alec remains in his chair, partly because it's so comfortable, partly because he really needs to process Donny's revelation. Roused by Andrew's slightly annoyed reminder that the room needs to be cleared, he shuffles his way back to his room. On the way he sees that Donny has caught up with two of the youngest lads and appears to be giving them a sneak preview of the glory that is contained in his trousers.

'I just don't see it' says Alec aloud to the empty corridor. Then another thought follows it. Perhaps you have to start when you are very, very young. This thought brings with it such gloom that Alec can barely be present in drawing class. Even when the tutor calls for volunteers and two of the more athletic men in the room enthusiastically volunteer to pose. Alec has never been able to progress in drawing beyond a slightly sophisticated stick figure and he is too ashamed to share his drawings with the group. There is some good-natured joshing about which parts of the body the group has rendered authentically, and which they have wildly exaggerated, but overall the morning is rather flat for Alec.

Still, he thinks, if I can get to the lunch first then I can save a place next to me for Donny. Leaving the group discussion at the end, which centres round one of the young men stimulating himself so as to more resemble his drawing likeness, Alec is first in the dining room. Unfortunately, when Donny enters it's with a group of young, admiring men, with whom Donny elects to dine. Donny's mellifluous voice booms out, followed by spontaneous yet, to Alec's jaundiced ears, sycophantic and artificial laughter. Alec is uncomfortably aware that he is again marooned on his metaphorical island. Then he senses movement next to him and is greatly pleased when Andrew drops his plate in the space next to him.

'Mind if I join you?' asks Andrew with an air of someone who has never known rebuke.

'Of course not, delighted, delighted' says Alec, irritated by his own over-enthusiasm.

‘First time here?’ asks Andrew.

‘Very first’ says Alec. ‘In fact, almost the very first anywhere. I did, a couple of weeks ago, have what you might from the outside consider a homosexual encounter. Take it from me, it was dreadful.’

‘So you’re still technically a virgin?’

‘I have had a child so I believe it would be more proper to say that I am spiritually a virgin.’

‘Good for you coming here. How are you finding it?’

There issues from Donny’s admirers a particularly raucous appreciation of his apparent wit.

‘Pretty bewildering’ Alec admits. ‘It’s not what I expected.’

‘I understand’ responds Andrew. ‘When I was married, I never thought my life would turn out like this. I thought marrying would save me from a lonely and sordid life. It’s only after my wife found out and we divorced and I found my way into this place that I realised the lonely and sordid life was the one I left.’

Alec stares at Andrew. He can’t be more than 28.

‘However old you are’ says Alec sincerely, ‘you’re still a child. You still have your whole life before you.’

‘I can say the same to you’ says Andrew. ‘Some relationships last many years, some a week, some a couple of hours. I know you may be thinking it’s all too late, but just think of living your real life within a limited time frame. Still time enough to fall in love, to experience complete physical fulfilment, perhaps to get your heart broken. Time to start the next one, and the one after that.’

Alec is aware that his eyes have filled with tears and that his hand is shaking with what he trusts is hope, not Parkinson’s.

'I do hope you're right, Andrew. I do so hope you're right.'

After lunch there's time for a walk or a rest. Alec knows he will regret not having a rest but Donny seems to be suddenly chatty so the two men go for a walk together. Donny is the sort who likes to entertain, and his material consists of a constant stream of descriptions of sex Donny has had, when, what, with whom, how many times, and whether it was or was not as good as all other previous times. After a while Alec, enjoying the movement of his limbs along the pleasant sandy path, is able to screen out most of Donny's monologue. Only the odd word floats into Alec's distracted mind.

'Sailor .... Bunk beds ... foursome...' Alec nods and smiles encouragingly although Donny needs no encouragement. After twenty minutes Alec feels overcome by a wave of tiredness and yawns in Donny's face. Donny yawns back and the two men retrace their steps and go to their separate rooms. On a whim Alec secretly follows Donny and is amazed to observe, as Donny opens his own door with the key, that a perfectly delightful young man has apparently been awaiting Donny's return. Shaking his head in dazed amazement Alec returns to his own room but there is no delightful surprise awaiting him.

After dinner the evening relaxes even further into a level of mellowness so pervasive and profound it could be marketed as mood candles. There is a sense of both exhilaration and sadness about the night still to unfold and the morning to follow. Sunday morning means the end of the weekend at Blythe. Trains will depart, cars will fill and leave, and by lunchtime the whole estate will be deserted. Tonight, if anything is going to happen, is the night. Alec, filled with both a dull tingling like a wobbly tooth, and a gentle melancholy like the end of his unblemished schooldays, half-listens while Donny concludes the arrangements for a shared bath with one of the most breath-taking members of the room. Andrew calls the room to order and asks if anyone has anything they would like to share with the group.

Someone stands and explains that he has come on the weekend to get over his latest breakup. He wants to thank the group for being there for him. Alec is bemused as to where else the group could be, yet the approving murmurs and applause that greets this rather fatuous, in Alec's opinion, contribution indicates that the young man apparently knows the right words for the occasion. Someone else stands and says that they came to the weekend with one boyfriend and they are leaving with another. This gets louder applause. Another man, Alec reckons about 40, says he's never come to a weekend like this but he'll be coming back again. This also gets a big hand. Something about the marvellous acceptance of every man in the room begins to have an effect on Alec. He's never been good at public speaking, the annual Board is a nightmare, yet in this room he suddenly feels he has the silver tongue of a particularly loquacious nightingale. He now waits impatiently for the current speaker, a man with short, auburn hair and spots, to finish. This speaker's contribution is that he always hated his spots, because they were a constant reminder of his failure to marry and make his parents happy, but thanks to the naked encounter he at last believes his body is beautiful. There is a roar at this and Alec finds himself having leapt to his feet, but having to wait for the applause to die down. When it does Alec feels all the eyes of the room turning to him.

'Uh' he says, cursing himself for not having jotted down something helpful beforehand. Spontaneity is not his forte.

'As some of you may know, I am a virgin.' If there's one thing the group appreciates more than sexually oriented contributions it's dry, almost Cowardian wit. Not realising that Alec is being honest, not amusing, the room rocks with laughter and they prepare for his next zinger.

'I would very much like to have sex with someone in this room. If anyone is interested, I'm in Room 24 on the second floor. I'll leave the door on the latch.'

There is a stunned silence. Andrew, earlier, thought he could leave Alec to make his own way through the invisible, unspoken but always stringent rules of gay men's social intercourse. Now he sees he should have considered more deeply what Alec was implying about the innocence of his state. Now, feeling the disapproval of the room at such an overt and crude announcement, sensing the judgment of 65 gay men, often critical and never more so than in the present, he feels a strange numbness. He begins to speak, to try to put Alec's words in some sort of context, but he can't think of a context other than that Alec has exposed his terrifying neediness to the group.

Alec has been expecting something along the lines of the cheery responses to the other contributors. To his rising horror he understands that he has, basically, stood up at the front of the room, dropped his trousers, and wagged his genitals in the combined faces of the attendees. And that his genitals are as unwelcome, and odorous, as Jerry's from a couple of weeks back.

The silence in the room is threatening to take actual physical form and violently eject Alec from the shocked throng. Then a little voice pipes up.

'That's the nicest thing anyone's said to me all weekend.' There is a mutter of disbelief and disapproval as all eyes, in one mass movement like a Mexican wave, swivel from Alec and in the direction of the new voice. Alec recognises the speaker as Zac, the young man from the muesli incident at breakfast. 'Let me know if you want a shared bath first and I'll put our names down on the list' Zac continues.

The rules of homosexual social discourse are strict but fair. If someone exposes their neediness and unlovability to the group it's nothing personal, it's only that neediness may be catching, and so that person is exposed and humiliated because no one is willing to join the pariah in pariahville. However, the situation changes sharply if anyone who is clearly a member of the desirable gay group declares an interest in the pariah. Then the pariah becomes, even if only temporarily, part of the larger, desirable group. It's basically the same rule that Donny has been exploiting for a great many years.

'Thank you' Alec manages to say. 'I think we can do without the bath. I've already had a shower.'

This strikes the group as deliberate, definitely Cowardian, and hugely hilarious. The whole room rocks with laughter and Donny gives Alec a proud wink out of his remaining eye. As the group splits into smaller cells Donny leans over to Alec.

'I'm proud of you. You've sat at my knee and listened to the master. I hope you enjoy whatever's coming.'

Unfortunately for those interested in prurient descriptions of passionate lovemaking, nothing much ensues. Zac explains that due to having had an unfortunate encounter with a metal object in his rectum he's unable to perform sexually. Instead, the two sit quietly on Alec's bed and talk about issues of interest to gay men. Alec explains his personal background. Zac explains that he's normally a highly sexed masseur and that he has come on the weekend in the hope of finding someone to replace his last lover, whilst taking a break from actual action.

'What was his name?' asks Alec, as one does, leaning against the bedhead and admiring, for the tenth time, the delicacy of Zac's mouth and thick lashes.

'Jerry' answers Zac artlessly.

The name Jerry causes Alec to shudder involuntarily and Zac looks concerned. 'Are you in a draft?'

'No. It's just that I recently encountered a Jerry. Couldn't have been your Jerry, this man … well, was very odd.'

Zac doesn't want to talk about 'his' Jerry either, so the co-incidence sails by the two men like a particularly odorous tramp steamer in the night.

'Have you come to one of these before?' asks Alec.

'Naah. Expensive. Only here this weekend because a punter suddenly couldn't make it. Gave me his booking. For this whole weekend I've had to remember my name is Raymond.'

After a while the two fall into a delightful doze. Later Zac wakes from it, instantly panicked that he is missing some of the night's other delights.

'But I thought you weren't having sex?' asks a puzzled and sleepy Alec.

'There's lots of other things!' responds Zac, checking in the mirror to see if he still looks 19.

'Could I have your number?' asks Alec.

Zac looks at Alec with honest eyes. 'I go for a guy about 50. We should have met 30 years ago.'

'Only 22' says Alec, indignantly.

'Whatever' says Zac. 'Thanks for the chat and the sleep.'

Ale doesn't try to stop Zac leaving. The door closes politely behind him. Alec listens to the night noises, the excited laughter, the sudden meaningful calm, the splashes from the bathroom. He knows he had a narrow escape. There was a moment in the big group when if he had been near a convenient precipice, he would have hurtled himself over its cruel edge without a second's debate. Yet someone came along and rescued him. That someone, even now, was no doubt making the acquaintance of a number of other eligible men. And that is probably as it should be. On the other hand, it cannot be denied that Alec had definitely spoken up in public. Had made his needs visible and immediate. And he hadn't gone over the edge. There had been someone there to reach out, to breach the mighty space that exists between Alec and the outside world. If it has happened once, he considers, surely it can happen again. It's like buying a house. The first one or two you like but there's always something wrong. It's only the third or fourth, or the 20th that's right. However, if there's one then there's twenty, and one of them will fit. On this hard-won yet satisfyingly correct thought Alec surrenders to the lure of the clean sheets and cosy blankets. Throughout the night men of all ages, sizes and wants course up and down the staircases and corridors of Blythe Hall, like so many randy corpuscles travelling through the body electric. Yet on this night too Alec sleeps all the way through. And in a strange way, he is still as much a part of it all as the other, various seekers covering every inch of night with their warm, whispered desires.

Eleven. ZAC and DARRYL and JERRY

On Sunday morning Zac packs carefully. To the purloined muesli he adds an eight-pack of assorted yoghurts, salt and pepper dispensers, six cloth napkins, jars of honey, jam and marmalade, a bowl of assorted dried fruits and six knives, forks and spoons. To ensure nothing jingles, once he is back in his room he wraps the entire haul in two of the hand towels. Rather than joining in the hours of sad, sweet farewells and introspection he persuades a delivery truck to drop him at the railway station.

On the way back to Soho Zac is hoping that in his absence Darryl, goaded into action by the lack of food in the flat, will have sorted out some new accommodation. His heart sinks when the moment he steps into his little world he sees Darryl sitting in the only chair.

'Did you have fun?'

Zac carefully places his rucksack on the table in the kitchenette. 'Yes' he sighs.

'Do you want more fun?'

Zac casts a questioning, dubious look in Darryl's direction.

'Look' croons Darryl softly, opening his hand, the acrylic nails catching the light and displaying a number of purple tablets. 'The answer to all problems, from flood to fire, hunger to poverty. Two of these tossed down with champagne and you'll feel like you've just bagged the last available Royal.'

'What are they?' asks Zac cautiously, mindful of the time he took tablets at a club and was found 12 hours later wedged in a shelf under the reception desk. It had been, he reflects, some 15th birthday.

‘Oh, nothing fatal’ says Darryl blithely. ‘I made my dealer take one in front of me and he was perfectly able to leave on his own two feet.’

‘So gimme’ says Zac, thinking that perhaps having Darryl around isn’t an entirely painful situation.

‘Not yet. I’m planning a special evening. Not only these little darlings, but I’ve got the name of the world’s greatest fortune teller.’

Like most people who live constantly on the edge, Zac craves the kind of security that comes only from paying a complete stranger to tell you entirely unsubstantiated yet strangely reassuring facts about love, wealth and career.

‘Sick!’ he pronounces. ‘Where is she?’

‘She’s really exclusive. Doesn’t advertise her address. No phone number. See the idea is you sail out into the night armed with her name. And if it’s right that you should meet her, then there is no power on earth that can prevent that happening.’

‘Wow’ says Zac. ‘So it really has to be a mystical meeting involving the cosmos and the fourth dimension and the da Vinci Code?’

Darryl smiles indulgently. ‘We do have some clues. She’s always in Coucous from 12.30pm and she eats in the Leicester Square McDonalds at 2am.’

‘Amazing.’

‘Yeah, and I called Jerry.’

Zac frowns.

‘Now don’t play miss drizzly face, I owed him. He always makes out I’m such a sponge. So I’ve invited him over for pills and fortune telling. All at my expense.’

'But I don't know if I want to see him' mutters Zac.

Darryl gives Zac an affectionate punch on the arm. 'You're not still moping over Jerry, are you? Look at you. You're beautiful. If he's not the right one, don't give him another second's thought. The right man is waiting for you out there.'

'How can I not give him a second thought if we're meeting tonight?'

Darryl extends his hand and opens it to again reveal the purple pills.

'Don't forget you'll have taken two of these. It will change your perspective on *everything*, I guarantee.'

Later, after Zac has seen to a punter and Darryl has burned his week's salary online, they get ready for the special night and quit the flat.

'I didn't know you were coming too' is Jerry's friendly greeting to Zac.

Flying on the tablets Zac merely smiles back, his eyeballs rotating like Catherine wheels. As the three set off to find the fortune teller Zac is filled with a sense of purpose, of a mythical, magical quest. Strange to relate, Zac's independence and confidence has a positive effect on Jerry. He wonders if he's made a bit of a mistake. The disadvantage of living in the margins as a sex worker is that every now and then all you want is a quiet chat and cuddle with someone you can trust. People outside the sex industry don't really understand those who are a part of it. Jerry has lost count and become entirely disenchanted with 'straight' boyfriends who, inevitably, want him to give up the sex trade and retrain as a shop assistant, road sweeper or long-distance lorry driver. Zac on the other hand was always understanding and willing to make compromises. While these thoughts are drifting through Jerry's mind he raises his glass of champagne and tosses down the purple tablets. After that, Jerry is not able to think period so his ruminations about Zac drift off with the rest of his thinking apparatus.

The three weave their wired way though Soho. It's still a little early to look for the fortune teller so they make bets on who can get free drinks for them all. Zac is well ahead by the end of the evening, although Jerry is still popular with a smaller, specialist category of benefactor. Darryl, able to move from place to place and never contribute as much as a fiver, is an old and practised hand at getting a round of free drinks. The evening passes in a wash of donated alcohol and chemically induced revelations about life and love.

As much fun as they are having no one has forgotten their quest for the fortune teller. The effects of the tablets coursing through their bloodstream, though, make it more and more difficult for them to construct the kind of focused, probing questions that would point them in the right direction. By midnight the three are so removed from even the living dreamworld of Soho that they begin to think in terms of bed and sleeping rather than inviting the fortune teller to probe deeply into their fried brain cells. So they totter off in the direction of their different homes, with Zac assisting Darryl and Jerry hopping onto one of the bicycle taxis that have added to the urban hazards of the West End.

Round about the same time that the fortune teller is standing in the queue at McDonalds and ordering a double cheeseburger and fries with a smoothie, the three are drifting into a childlike sleep. At the time none of them is aware that sometimes there can be unexpected consequences to too much champagne mixed with too many pills. In this instance, that by not hearing the fortune teller they are robbed of the chance of being warned. Doubtless they would have been quickly sobered to learn from the fortune teller that within a short period, perhaps as few days as a week, one of them would be in an accident that, although not entirely fatal for them personally, would still involve a life-changing experience.

Twelve. SANDRA

Sandra, sitting as per usual behind her work desk, stretches and yawns. It's been a long day and she still has a couple of hours to put in before she can look forward to a quick drink and then home. She sweeps a pile of dreary papers into a folder, stands and quickly strides down the corridor to Alec's office. She admires the genuine 19th century oak panelling, the antique desk behind which his PA sits, the family portraits that give the chairman's office gravitas and grandeur and thinks that one day soon she will be but one person away from all this. She already has a plot in mind to dispose of Dennis.

She sees, as she expects, that Rochelle is at her usual post, guarding the door to Alec's office. She pictures the room inside. More of the impressive original panelling, more family portraits mixed with a few St Ives 20th Century paintings of excellent quality, plus the antique Persian carpets which reduce all sound in the space to an elegant whisper. Her nipples grow hard with desire.

Looking down at where Rochelle sits Sandra realises her nipples are remaining extended and voluptuous. She idly scratches the area through her bra and gasps with pleasure. Rochelle, hearing the unfamiliar sound, looks up. The eyes of the two women meet.

'I recognised you by your gasp' says Rochelle.

Sandra sits on a corner of Rochelle's desk. She reaches out and grasps Rochelle's hand. 'You work too hard' she replies. Sandra gently pulls Rochelle's hand up to Sandra's face. She opens her red-lipsticked mouth and gently inserts Rochelle's fingers. Now it's Rochelle's turn to gasp. Rochelle rises and throws her body against Sandra's.

'I've always desired, I never dreamed' Rochelle whispers in a cloud of expensive perfume. The heady atmosphere is causing Sandra's mind to whirl, yet she is also entirely in control. She pushes Rochelle against the panelling and Rochelle gasps again as the hard wood connects with her tender flesh. Sandra begins to reach under Rochelle's skirt, moving her grasping fingers higher and higher, finally gaining the forbidden territory, learning to her delighted surprise that Rochelle is going commando, is gloriously sporting a perfect Sharon Stone…!

Sandra wakes up in the privacy and darkness of her bedroom. She takes in the hushed quiet, the faint dawn straining to peep through the blackout curtains, the beeping of her alarm clock.

'Well. That was interesting' she thinks. In the shower she finds herself unconsciously playing with her nipples while recalling the moment before she woke. She sips her morning coffee, holding onto the feeling of happiness in the dream. When did she last feel some emotion towards another person? At the beginning of her career Sandra had decided that she was not going to be like most of the Lesbians she knew. She was not going to declare herself, and then suffer through the years of snide looks, *double entendres*, supposed witticisms. She was not going to be included or excluded as one of the boys. She knew about the secret deals done in the men's room specifically to keep her out the loop.

So, as she rose up through the corporate ladder, she would drop a hint here and there, just enough to keep the wolves from baying at her desk. Her latest camouflage was feigning an interest in the elderly walrus and she was pleased to observe it was gaining traction. Yet here she has been betrayed by her own subconscious.

There is, she observes, only one positive aspect to the matter. No one else knows. No one else has looked through the window into her mind. At work she can still drop Alec's name into a conversation and not feel her audience is laughing behind their hands. Her insight into her inner feelings will remain a discreet, passionate memory. While on the outside she will continue to live the pretence of her life. The idea of 'coming out' she has always dreaded.

As she enters her executive office, she is startled by an image that seems left over from her dream. Rochelle is in her office, leaning over and picking up some papers dropped on the floor. From Sandra's perspective she sees Rochelle's magnificently curved thighs and derriere, and for a mad moment Sandra wonders if she's still sleeping and if it's permissible to reach out two carefully manicured hands and grasp glorious handfuls of Rochelle's creamy body.

Startled by a gasp Rochelle rears up abruptly and her sensuous mouth curves in a heartfelt apology.

'Sorry to startle, Sandra! I just dropped these …'

Conscious of her wildly beating heart, Sandra does not trust herself to speak. Instead she shakes her head, flaps her hand in gestures she hopes Rochelle will understand. Rochelle speedily quits Sandra's room, although her perfume remains, a heady atmosphere for Sandra to breath in deeply and enjoy.

All through the day, for one reason or another, Rochelle keeps muscling her way back into Sandra's awareness. Try as she may to completely erase the sight, the sound, the scent, so for some bedevilled reason Rochelle keeps needing to have a quick word, to check, to verify, to get Sandra to sign.

By 5pm Sandra is fit to be tied, run round the paddock and put to bed with a warm rub down and a Native American blanket. She is incapable of concentrating on any of a dozen urgent business matters. There comes to her the awful image of what it will be like, once she has entirely given up on the day, to go home to her comfortable but very lonely apartment. A minute later, seemingly accomplished without the aid of her conscious mind, Sandra finds her footsteps leading her towards Rochelle's little office. She pauses in the doorway and Rochelle, still battling with the day's correspondence, looks up and greets her with a gentle, intimate, smile.

'I was wondering' says Sandra, wondering what she's going to say next. 'Wondering?'

Rochelle's smile of greeting becomes slightly tarnished by the thought that Sandra has worked so hard that her mind is unravelling. Rochelle knows that she would find it difficult to continue at Bland & Co without Sandra there to lift the tedium of her days. She hopes there's more.

'Wondering if you were thinking about a drink before home?' asks Sandra in a single breath out.

Rochelle's face lights up and Sandra realises that when she's given the opportunity to smile, Rochelle looks a little like the beautiful 1940s film star Gene Tierney. She wonders how Rochelle would look in black and white, then becomes aware that Rochelle has answered.

'What?'

'I'd love to have a drink with you.'

Sandra has become involved in an inner musing on whether Rochelle really does look like Gene Tierney, or whether her nose doesn't in fact point more towards Jennifer Lawrence. Rochelle repeats her acceptance of Sandra's suggestion and the two beam happily and silently at each other for a beat or two.

Then Sandra, realising that as the initiator and as higher up in the corporate ladder the onus is on her to complete the arrangements, names seven pm as the time when she will drop by Rochelle's office to pick her up.

Wafting back along the corridor to her office Sandra's face carries such a smirk of dazed happiness that one of the middle managers congratulates her on being pregnant. Sandra reverts to her usual work persona and tears the hapless employee a new one.

'I've always looked inside this place. But never wanted to come in on my own.'

This is Rochelle speaking. Sandra has been to the bar and now places two glasses of red wine on the white tablecloth.

'I know what you mean' says Sandra. 'By the time I leave I'm always too knackered to fight through the crowd at the bar.'

'Yes. Mind you I've been in here once or twice. When it was a birthday or someone leaving,'

Sandra raises her glass and lightly touches Rochelle's in a delicate toast.

'It's pathetic how little we ask of ourselves' she declares thoughtfully. 'I remember once a colleague telling me that, since they were going to Sydney on business, they were going to make sure that this time they had a drink from the hotel room mini-bar. Imagine flying 14,000 miles for a little glass bottle of Walkers.'

The combination of the most desirable woman in the world sitting opposite her, and a rare insight into the corporate delusion regarding which she is an enthusiastic and usually uncritical rat, causes Sandra's eyes to mist over. Rochelle's lovely eyes take on an expression of infinite gentleness and sweet sympathy.

'You're crying? Is it something I said?'

Sandra reaches out and grasps one of Rochelle's hands. It's so soft yet also, honed by countless hours of work on the keyboard, surprisingly firm and trustworthy. One little voice in Sandra's head is crying out for Sandra to remember that Rochelle is attached to the business world, you know, the world you determined would never know the truth about you. While another voice, gentler and more supportive, notes merely that Rochelle has not pulled her hand away.

'Isn't it sad about Alec's wife' says Rochelle. Sandra is so advanced in her fantasy about her and Rochelle, a beach, moonlight and all the free drinks on the island, that for a moment she's about to say 'Who?' before Rochelle's words drag her back to the bar.

'Yes. Awful' she says automatically, while her eyes trace the line of Rochelle's neck, down, down until it's lost in the suggestion of cleavage and buried in her sensible work blouse. 'I wish I knew how I could help.'

'Well' says Rochelle, her voice resuming its usual practical tone. 'I could send some stuff your way so he wouldn't always have to deal with the minutia. He trusts me enough to let me decide what's going to happen with most of the correspondence.'

Sandra has sunk into a mini-reverie of Rochelle lying face upwards on the bar while Sandra licks Courvoisier, Baileys and Crème de Menthe off her naked torso. But she is essentially a boardroom animal and at the sound of this her vision fades and her mind grinds into gear.

'You mean it? You could … let me in on what's going on?'

Rochelle's eyes widen with surprise. 'But you know what's going on, don't you?'

Sandra thinks with lightning speed. 'Oh *yes*, I mean, I'm Operations Manager. But there's a lot of … strategic … that I get left out of. Where really it could only help Alec if I know …' and here the phrase she's grasping for, as she knows, is 'if I had all the sensitive information that's right now kept secret.' Even though Rochelle seems to be enjoying her glass inordinately Sandra is still aware of the importance of not giving the game away.

'If I know whatever would be helpful' she concludes vaguely. Let Rochelle take the blame for anything top secret Alec didn't want her to know about.

Then Sandra's chest catches, drawing her attention back to her last thought. Could she actually betray Rochelle? Lovely Rochelle? Surely not. Yes she's ambitious, but at the cost of harming her new level of personal intimacy with Rochelle? Soberly Sandra registers that she hopes she will never have to find out.

'I'm afraid I've got to run' says Rochelle a few minutes later.

'Me too' says Sandra, forever competitive.

On the street Sandra allows Rochelle to have the first taxi. As Rochelle begins to get into the taxi she turns back, about to remind Sandra of some work-related trivia. Misinterpreting, Sandra leans slightly down, opens her mouth, and embraces Rochelle in such a manner that there is no room for doubt as to her sexual agenda. Rochelle hurriedly retracts herself and a flash of horror courses through Sandra. 'Betrayed! By my own lust!' she gasps internally.

'Eh.... Thank you, Sandra. That was ... great...The wine. Delicious' Rochelle manages to stammer out before she throws herself into the security of the taxi and slams the door. Like a fool, like a spurned suitor, like a woman who has gone far too far with a work colleague and would now like to bite herself hard, Sandra can only stand, dumbfounded at her own stupidity as the taxi crawls its way into the stream of traffic.

For a long minute Sandra stands where she is, in the road, shielded from passing vehicles by standing between two parked cars. Then even her slim shroud of self-possession leaves her like fleas deserting a sinking dog and she howls into the pitiless street.

'What have I done?! How could I be so indiscreet!' And even more scary: what will Rochelle tell everyone at the office tomorrow?

Thirteen. ALEC & GUY

Farewells on a Sunday morning at Blythe Hall tend to be exhaustively emotional events. Alec goes along with the crowd, and soon gets the hang of clutching someone whose name you evidently don't remember but who will nevertheless give you a full body embrace and a sloppy kiss. Indeed, his tally of these encounters quickly rises into double figures. However, the journey home from Blythe is unexpectedly difficult, at least internally, at least for Alec. Although the younger members of the weekend mark the ending with a light laugh followed by a deep plunge into Grindr, Alec's feelings are many and complex. For 36 hours he has lived as he has always desperately desired to, at one with a large body of men all of similar if not identical persuasions. Faced with the gloom of returning to Bland's and the bleakness of his large, empty house, Alec wonders if he should just turn around? Perhaps he can beg the powers that be at Blythe hall to allow him to assist the groundsman? Surely being in at least geographical proximity to that wellspring of gay happiness is better than all the expense lunches, the power meetings, the cosy fires in his library, crowded in by books written by dead, heterosexual men? Of course it is, yet Alec lacks the self-confidence to propose to Andrew that he push a wheel-barrow round the kitchen garden. He's never been given a plant that hasn't wilfully died on him. The ability to distinguish flowers from weeds spitefully eludes him.

So, he resolves with a sigh, it is back to London, to reality, to a wretched existence. Livened, he then reminds himself, by his having met Donny. And Zac. At the name, an image of the lad's face floats into his mind's eye and at the image his heart misses a beat. Recognising that this was no revisit of his valve problem, Alec wonders with a special awe if it is actually possible for a man to feel about another man the way a man is supposed to feel towards women. Yes, he had along the years encountered two men together, yet without being able to question them deeply on what they felt for each other he'd always just assumed it was purely lust. But this feeling he is developing for Zac isn't located in his middle, but in that place where the worth of a person is found. The rest of the day is taken up with these and similarly sentimental fancies. Somehow, perhaps because he is conscious of a new energy beginning to form inside him, he is also able to get through a considerable amount of extremely tedious Bland's work. Alec also puts in a call to Guy, asking him for another appointment, implying on the phone that he has something of a minor revelation to impart.

Guy puts down the phone from Alec with a grunt of satisfaction. He wasn't sure that he had said and done the right things with Alec. With someone so unfamiliar with their internal workings, with someone who has his whole life pushed down and denied his feelings, coming to therapy can be too great a challenge and attack on their equilibrium. Alec, though, sounded bouncy and infused with a passion to progress and Guy is pleased he appears to have an ongoing commitment to therapy.

Guy is still embroiled in the hardest aspect of a relationship: the break-up. Ted has been on a couple of dates with other men but swears that nothing happened during them. Conversely, meeting the new men has driven him back into Guy's unwilling arms with even greater force than before. It seems to be something of a cupid's joke that the more Guy attempts to get through to Ted that he can no longer supply his emotional and sexual needs, the more Ted appears to need both and in ever-increasing quantities. Guy sits alone, sips coffee, thinks dark and gloomy thoughts. If he cannot find a way to convince Ted to detach and move out, he is going to feel ever more trapped and unfit to live a full life. Which will inevitably have an effect on his performance as a therapist and the whole vicious cycle will spiral ever further downward until he becomes one of those therapist's he's always despised: those who say nothing because they have nothing to say.

Until, in the depths of internal angst, Guy realises he has been neglecting 50% of the potential for effecting a break-up.

'I'll meet someone new!' cries Guy. Since he's always focused on the other person, the idea that he can unilaterally decide to have something for himself really is a revelation. 'Ted can't keep throwing himself into my arms if someone new is already in them!'

And, as he knows from his extensive clinical reading but also from his devoted reading of Reddit, the fundamental reason for many break ups is that one of the parties finds someone else. After that it's just a matter of drawing up legal documents and dividing the household.

Within an online hour Guy has met, chatted to, and agreed to meet a new young man for drinks at 7pm. He also agrees to meet another young man and go with him to a friend's loft party. Guy wouldn't usually make two dates in an evening but working freelance he has always saved his evenings for clients. It's only due to a beneficial brace of cancelled sessions that he is free this one evening. Guy even attempts to make a third date for after-show coffee just to prove to himself how serious he is.

Leaving Ted a note in which he is extremely vague about the time he can be expected home, Guy completes his clients sessions and notes, showers, does a quick body-hair whip round with his electric razor and dresses carefully. Since Guy's playtime wardrobe consists almost entirely of figure-hugging T-shirts, not a lot of thought is required. The evening is warm enough to complete the outfit with just a casual linen jacket, appropriate for drinks, loft parties and whatever else comes his way.

'You wouldn't think it but I'm only 23' says the man sitting on a bar stool opposite Guy. Actually, thinks Guy, I wouldn't believe you were 30. I'm 50 and I don't have the wrinkles you have.

'I don't sleep with men on the first date' the man, Adrian, in soft furnishings, announces. 'I've found that if I sleep with the man on the first date then that's it. There's never a second.' Guy is surprised only that someone would need to sleep with Adrian before coming to this conclusion.

However, wanting to be a good sport, Guy listens for an hour while Adrian explains, in painful detail, the many joys of his particular leisure pass time: gay Western dancing.

'You can go to a boot scoot virtually any night in London' says Adrian. 'I make it a policy never, *never* to attend more than three nights a week. Otherwise you find yourself dancing with the same tired men. Instead when I'm not at the scoot, I'm at home with my feet up, or in a Radox bath, giving my face an all-over scrub and plucking out any stray nose, neck, ear or chest hairs.'

Adrian brings his face closer to Guy's, presumably so Guy can admire his handiwork.

'What time do you have to be up in the morning?' asks Adrian suddenly. Guy wonders how this can tally with his previous statement about not putting out on the first date. Guy could be accused of being unnecessarily presumptuous if not for the fact that at the same time Adrian has dropped his hand into Guy's crotch and is now rubbing vigorously. The discomfort causes Guy to jump to his feet, dislodging Adrian's advance party.

'Actually I've got a ton of work to do back home before I go to bed' says Guy.

'I can wait till you're finished. This girl knows when to be quiet' responds Adrian.

Guy hurriedly pays for their drinks, makes his way through the bar, gains with a sigh of relief the cool outside street. He begins to walk speedily in the direction of the tube. He needs to find his way to Surrey Quays and the loft party. After a minute he becomes aware that he has been trailing Adrian behind him. He stops.

'Sorry, Adrian, but I don't think we're right for each other.'

Adrian stands as though thunderstruck.

'But' he cries, 'I was willing to give you the key to my temple! And my temple attracts only the most exclusive worshippers!'

'Thanks, but I'm looking for something a little less complicated' Guy replies, as he walks swiftly away. Behind him he can hear Adrian, who appears to have confused a simple date for drinks with a lifetime's commitment and is for some peculiar reason threatening Guy with the police. *Please* thinks Guy, don't try to tell me you're underage! For a moment Guy considers what he has not had to deal with in the years he has been together with Ted. Ted, even now, does not behave like this.

Yet Guy also knows, at a deeper layer of thought, that Ted and he are no more. For them to stay together now would be preparing for a life of sexless friendship. Although that has its charms Guy, like St Augustine, believes 'give me celibacy, Lord, but not yet…'

Exiting the tube at Surrey Quays Guy searches discreetly for his second date of the night. This is a young man he believes he may have already met, if it's who he thinks it is. It was at the time he was having problems with his lower back. He contacted a couple of massage therapists. The first one gave a competent massage but was totally uninspiring. The second, who worked on his bed rather than a proper table, was physically very attractive and appealing, but not that great a manipulator. Until the end, which left Guy feeling *very* happy. In fact, rather than using one of the social media hook up sites, Guy has fished the man's card out of his wallet, explained that he doesn't want a massage but a date, and on getting an affirmative from the man, who says he does remember him, Guy feels a real sense of progress.

Fourteen. ALEC AND ZAC

Striding with unaccustomed vigour through the hallowed corridors of Bland & Co, Alec wonders if anyone will comment on the difference the weekend has made to him. He pauses by the staff bulletin board to read a postcard from receptionist Jenny. She notes that she is enjoying her holiday in Tenerife, entirely on the company's dime, and finishes with a vague threat to do something they will regret if her time away is in any way prematurely curtailed. Not understanding anything Jenny has carefully encrypted in her neat handwriting, Alec gives her no further thought as he catches up with his senior staff.

A while later finds Alec puzzled. Although it's he who has had the revelatory weekend, it seems to be the others who have changed. Dennis has adopted a waspish arrogance and Sandra seems to be giving herself the most complicated and elaborate alibi. For what Alec has yet to determine. His own PA, the rock of the workplace, Rochelle, is also behaving oddly. She seems to be conducting an ongoing inner argument either with herself or some nameless other. However, a quick call to Zac, a brief exchange concluding with a day and time to drop by his flat, and Alec feels more grounded. That the day is today and the time 5pm also helps.

Pressing on Zac's doorbell at exactly 5pm, Alec is surprised to find the door answered by the man who he last saw in that dreadful man Jerry's flat.

'Hello' says the man. 'I'm Darryl, remember? I must say you do get around.'

Alec enters and Darryl shuts the door. Normally Alec would feel entirely tongue-tied but the effects of the weekend haven't completely worn off.

'I can say the same about you' says Alec, tartly.

'You could but on me it's only to expected' Darryl explains. 'I'm a perennial orphan of the storm, tossed from one unsafe harbour to the next. You on the other hand look like you don't even have a mortgage on your detached house, villa or mansion.'

This is true so Alec merely nods in sympathy of Darryl's very different circumstances. At that moment Zac enters from having washed his hands.

'Where's the table?' asks Alec in confusion.

'The bed's really comfortable' replies Darryl.

'We can do it on the floor?' asks Zac.

'Don't mind me, I'll just read a magazine' says Darryl. Alec exchanges a questioning look with Zac.

'Actually, Darryl, can you read your mag in some café? Or the park? It's not cold.'

Darryl makes a show of protest by rolling his eyes and sighing deeply. Yet he is too old a hand at the art of freeloading to know that he has no tenant's rights.

'I'm off. Don't do anything Tom Cruise wouldn't' is his parting shot. After Darryl has slammed the door Alec looks dubiously at the floor.

'Sorry, dear, I just cannot. I had a terrible encounter with a bean bag at the weekend. I know my limits.'

'Okay' says Zac with the fluidity of the young and philosophical. 'Sit on the bed. I'll go behind you and sort of use my elbows.'

Alec perches on the bed while Zac balances on the bed behind him. Alec begins to appreciate the pressure of Zac's elbow, massaging and separating out his tired, ageing muscles.

'This is delightful' he says after a few minutes.

'Great' says Zac.

After fifteen minutes Zac has run out of places to safely massage Alec. 'Alec,' he asks, 'can I tell you something kind of personal? I suppose that you're after what everyone else wants, a bit of slap and tickle at the end. Can I ask, can we just not?'

Alec pulls himself away from Zac and turns round as best he can, to see Zac's eyes are full of unaccustomed levity.

'You mean I'm that unlovable?' Asks Alec in a low sad tone.

'No, it's not exactly that. I mean you're no worse than other guys I've massaged. But there's something about you.'

'I know' says Alec gloomily. 'I'm some sort of eternal spinster, destined for purity and never passion.'

'No, it's not that. It's just that you're the spitting of my grandfather and, well, even us masseurs are human. We have our limits.'

'Oh' says Alec, a little brighter, 'Oh that's different. Yes, I can imagine you as a grandson. And frankly that has terminated any other feeling I might have been nurturing for you.'

'Awesome' says Zac. 'So shall I go make a cup of tea and we can talk about stuff generally?'

'Will you still expect me to pay you?'

'Of course not. But as grandad you might want to buy me a present for my birthday that's just gone.'

'I'm sorry I didn't know. When was it?'

'Five months ago.'

Although Alec is momentarily disappointed that Zac is going to take him no further along his erotic road, the idea that Zac finds in him a grandfather figure is also strangely appealing. He can imagine himself getting even older and ever more doddery and having Zac around to look after him. Since up till now he has been planning to leave his considerable estate to some estranged cousins, the idea that Zac could become his heir is highly appealing. He remembers reading that Jean Cocteau, the French surrealist artist, playwright and filmmaker did the same, adopting a handsome young man to be his heir and nurse.

'We should talk further' he says as Zac politely shoves him out the door. Zac had hitherto explained that he has a proper date for the evening.

'Of course, gramps' says Zac, then reconsiders. 'No, I'll still call you Alec. But I'll think of you as a grandfather.'

'And I'll consider you a grandson but call you Zac' says Alec.

'Actually, I'd prefer it if you called me Adam. That's my real name.'

'Very well' says Alec, pleased with this symbol of trust and intimacy.

In the street Alec hails a cab and waves to Adam, who walks off in the opposite direction.

Guy is glad he wore his jacket because now that the sun has gone the evening is slightly chilly. He is still waiting for Zac. He's beginning to think that he's been stood up, that perhaps Ted is still better than the vagaries of dating, when he hears a cheery call and turning, sees Zac approaching. That Zac has no sense of time is, of course, appealing to Guy's need to rescue and heal. He looks forward to teaching Zac to be more punctual. Zac throws his skinny yet strong arms around Guy and plants a kiss on Guy's open mouth. Having checked that none of the passers-by have a problem with that, Guy returns the embrace.

'You sure you need to go this party?' asks Guy. 'My place is only a taxi ride away.' He speaks confidently, knowing Ted has gone to visit one of his new Grindr friends for the night.

'Oh, yeah, Philip's like my bestie. And it'll be cool. He'll have spent some money. Not like some people who throw a party and you have to bring your own food and drinks' he adds, having suffered through a couple of Darryl's celebratory efforts.

'You're the boss' says Guy, slipping Zac a devastating smile. The two link arms and walk the short distance to Philip's borrowed loft space.

Climbing the two floors of cement steps they can hear loud, but not obnoxious, party sounds, a mixture of excited conversation and mellow music. Gaining entry they are hit by a wave of body warmth. Guy immediately feels a little claustrophobic. Zac gets drinks for two and they find a place in the melee.

'What?' asks Zac, becoming slightly irritated by Guy's constant sideways glances. 'Have I got something in my teeth? Visible nose hairs?'

Guy laughs and wraps a powerful arm around Zac's fragile body.

'Nothing like that. I mean, you are dangerously close to my definition of perfection.'

Zac is relieved and inordinately pleased to hear this. Even though he is still only 19, he has been his only resource for nearly five years. He has been used to finding his own way through life, to parlaying his meagre assets into enough to pay his modest way. He wouldn't exchange his life for Philip's solid, stable, boring existence, though. He lives on the edge and likes the view. Yet every now and then he dreams of an attractive older man who will stand next to him and whisper exactly this sort of reassurance into his eager ear.

'I hope I'll see a lot more of you. I don't mean to be funny. I mean, look. I'm just getting out of an important relationship,'

'Oh I get you' shouts Zac above the din. 'I mustn't get too hopeful.'

Guy looks deeply into Zac's eyes, seeing how quickly the pretty green circles fill with pain. He knows in this moment that he wants to be the one to wipe away all that distress.

'No, opposite! I hate being on my own. I don't care if Ted leaves tomorrow and you've got your moving van parked round the side. I'm not one for long engagements.'

Zac considers that there is still the matter of his professional gay status. Will Guy be okay with the idea or will Zac have to give up his lucrative fumblings?

'I have a couple of things I should tell you' shouts Zac.

'Oh. Okay. Like you already have a boyfriend and he's out of town tonight?'

'I wish! Nothing like that. First thing my name isn't Zac, it's Adam.'

Guy looks at Adam and smiles a wrinkly acceptance. 'Okay …'

'And there's something else. Bigger.'

At this juncture, with Adam aware of his own loudly beating heart forming a counter-rhythm with the music, they are joined by Philip. with Adam aware that his own loudly beating heart is forming a contra-rhythm to the music.

'So. This is the new man. Very tasty' pronounces Philip. Guy laughs.

'This is only our first date' says Guy.

'Yeah, but I've seen that look in his eye before. The guy didn't stand a chance.'

Guy laughs at this but Adam frowns, thinking that perhaps coming to the party was a bad idea. He wants to be in control of how the evening unfolds.

'Philip, happy birthday' shouts Adam and gives him a brotherly kiss 'in case we don't see you again.'

Philip takes the hint and moves off to talk to other friends. Adam gives Guy a searching look.

'Okay, so this bigger thing. I have to tell you now.'

'You're HIV positive?'

'No. And I have regular checks.'

'Okay. So what else can be that big?'

A group of merrymakers forming a spontaneous conga line bash into the couple. Adam grasps Guy's elbow, admiring the bicep beneath the jacket, remembering their first encounter and looking forward eagerly to the concluding section of the evening. He steers Guy in the direction of a solid wall between two huge windows of glass.

Actually, technically, the feature wall of the loft has three huge glass windows. The middle section can be divided and slid back. Someone, while setting up the party, has opened the middle windows and then, in deference to the slight chill but wanting to ensure sufficient air for the party, has pulled down a light canvas blind. To the uninitiated, the slightly inebriated and the distracted it would appear that the wall is solid. Solid enough to lean on. Yet since all there is behind the canvas is a low, brick wall, and then a huge expanse of defenestrated space, Adam and Guy are standing in front of a potential death trap.

Not that Adam is thinking about potential disasters. He knows that when he insists he be allowed to keep making money his particular way he will probably lose Guy. Prior to this there have been several occasions which began hopefully, with the man promising that nothing Adam could tell him would make a difference. Adam would get his hopes up, only to have them dashed by the look of fury, or bewilderment, or disgust in the face of his new paramour. Who shortly afterwards would become his latest failure.

So, with not much hope but with a real determination that he will be truthful, Adam begins. 'You know what I do, Guy. I bring happiness to as many people as I meet. With these hands. And sometimes other parts of my anatomy.'

Guy is laughing at the line and takes a beat to process. He looks quizzically at Adam.

'Are you telling me you want to keep working as a sex worker?'

Adam's eyes fill with tears. Another good one bites the dust he thinks. Adam anxiously scans Guy's face for signs of how the revelation is going down. Guy hasn't pushed him away or thrown his drink in his face, so that gets a tick. On the other hand he doesn't seem to be reacting at all. Only the rapid eye movements tell Adam that Guy is thinking furiously. Then Guy smiles.

'Okay. Sorry if I scared you. I wasn't thinking about you, really. I was thinking about a couple of sex workers I've had as clients. It doesn't surprise me that after my clients telling me about their lives, I now meet someone like you. Don't you think these things are like fate?'

'So you don't mind?' asks Adam in a voice so small it's immediately lost in the tumult of noise and party stomping.

'It's not that I mind. It's your life. I can't influence you.' Inside, of course, Guy is congratulating himself on having finally linked up with someone with what appears to be years of damage to unpick, to smooth out, to heal. Thinking further he's amazed he has never cottoned on to his own truest nature. Growing up the thing he admired most about the story of Jesus was how He was embracing of all, including and particularly the divine harlot Mary Magdalene. Ted had problems yet he was relatively easily able to move into a career of life insurance. Adam's choice of career, with the hundred daily abuses to which he exposes himself, lifts Guy's spirits to the heights. He can't wait to get out of this party and start showing Adam just how much he is okay with what Adam does for a living.

'I like you just as you are' he says sincerely. 'And I like you a lot.'

If someone had captured the moment on their phone, perhaps for an art exhibition held in the ground floor gallery in the very same building, they would call it '`Young Man Ecstatic.' Because that's how Adam feels, and looks. He has finally found the man of his dreams. A hunk, just the right age, and with a generous and accepting nature. In a spasm of joy Adam throws his arms around Guy and pushes him against the wall, the better to embrace him.

Except, as noted earlier, it's not a solid brick wall. With a material-whipping sound the fragile screed balloons away and out, exposing the room and the two men to the terrible night and a downward plunge to the street below. There is a tiny instant in which Guy realises he is falling backwards, then he and Adam begin a relentless drop towards the unwelcome concrete pavement. It has been observed that when we are in moments of crisis time appears to stand almost still. Guy is able to observe the looks of horror on the faces of those witnessing the disaster. He's able to feel Adam's warm body still wrapped around him and hear both his own cry and Adam's terrified scream. A natural carer to the end, he is even able to ensure that he will be the first to hit the ground, and perhaps his body will cushion the impact for Adam.

As it is, the impact of warm flesh and bone, with merciless concrete pavement, kills Guy instantly. Adam, with the benefit of landing on Guy, experiences an instant of sheer horror as he feels Guy exploding beneath him. Then he is engulfed by a pain greater than any other he has suffered as the impact shatters his leg, causing him to blackout.

Within a minute the street has filled with horrified party goers, a couple of whom cannot be made to stop screaming. A dozen phones summons ambulances and the other critical resources. The wail of police sirens competes with the hysteria of the stunned revellers. The only comfort Philip can take is that Guy isn't suffering and that Adam is still alive, although unconscious. An efficient female police officer begins taking witness statements. Philip gasps. Will he be held culpable for the madness of the window? Would they do that to him? He was only trying to ensure everyone got some air. He insists on accompanying Adam's ambulance to hospital, where he is treated gently, interviewed by the police, and allowed to return home where he cries himself to a tortured sleep.

Fifteen. ALEC & Co.

'For heaven's sake' mutters Alec. 'Has everyone here gone mad?'

A harsh judgement on his work colleagues, yet somewhat justified. In order to check an insignificant amount on one of the subsidiary monthly balance sheets, Alec has just attempted to get a straight answer out of Dennis. First he had to track Dennis down. Dennis, according to his PA Philip, was in the men's toilet.

Normally Alec, the most private of men, would not deliberately court the company of other men in the loo. Yet since Blythe Hall he has begun to adopt a more relaxed attitude towards casual nudity and bodily functions. He can't see anything wrong with sticking his head round the door of the Men's and asking Dennis a quick question.

Ordinarily he would merely have asked Philip to get Dennis to see him when he had a moment. Philip, though, seems seized with some internal distress that has reduced his usual sunny countenance to a weeping, red-eyed picture of grief. He wonders if he should insist that Philip be sent home. He supposes he could include the question in his discussion with Dennis. Who does not appear to be coming out of the Men's any time soon. So Alec takes a deep breath and pushes the door open.

Expecting to see only Dennis's shoes, and perhaps a neat folding of pants, under one of the toilet stalls, Alec is surprised to see that Dennis is not so much using the facilities as cleaning them.

'My dear man' says Alec. 'We have people to do that.'

Dennis looks up from his task. His brow glistens with sweat and his eyes are wide and infused with an intimidating gleam.

‘They’ he answers, putting all his strength into lifting a particularly stubborn stain from one of the basins, ‘don’t get all the muck off. It drives me crazy.’

Alec stares at Dennis a moment.

‘Something I can do for you?’ asks Dennis, emitting a satisfied grunt as the stain gives up the struggle.

‘Oh, just a question about the … never mind.’ Alec begins to close the door when he has another thought and pushes it open.

‘I say. Your PA. Seems to be having a rough day.’

Dennis turns on the hot tap and water gushes merrily into the now spotless basin.

‘Keep your nose out’ he snaps.

‘Really, no need to take that tone. I’m merely acknowledging that your PA seems to be in distress.’

‘If he wanted to go home he’d ask me. Perhaps he likes having other people around? Perhaps they distract?’

‘All the same…’ says Alec although he knows he’s reached the limit of his empathy towards another human being.

‘Stay out’ snaps Dennis.

Alec allows the door to gently close and goes off to ask Sandra about the tiny error on the balance sheet. She isn’t behind her desk, so Alec asks Rochelle if she’s seen her. To his dismay Rochelle’s head snaps up and there’s a look of undeniable panic in her usually serene eyes.

‘Why would I have seen Sandra? Why would you think we’re unnaturally close?’

Alec, of course, has no greater meaning behind his question other than the usual vague belief that someone must know.

‘I can’t find her anywhere’ explains Alec, electing not to comment on Rochelle’s demeanour.

‘She must be somewhere’ responds Rochelle. ‘Perhaps she’s gone for a walk.’

Alec knows both that Sandra never leaves the office during waking hours, and also that Rochelle’s wild speculation doesn’t merit reply. Instead he proffers what he thinks is a sensible suggestion.

‘She’s probably in the Ladies. Dennis seems to have started a new career in the Men’s. Why don’t you look for her in the Ladies?’

‘Oh!’ says Rochelle, snatching up a pile of papers as though to give the appearance of being snowed under with paperwork. ‘Oh but why would you think I would want to see Sandra in the Ladies? I mean we don’t have that sort of relationship. Has anyone been talking to you? Has Sandra?’

It is at this point that Ale concludes that everyone in the office has lost their way mentally.

‘I don’t know what you mean. When you see Sandra, can you ask her to have a word with me?’

‘What word? Tell me and I’ll tell you if it’s true!’ cries Rochelle.

Alec shakes his head and returns to his own office. He sits behind his executive desk and fishes out his phone. Five times in the last 48 hours he has called and left messages on Adam’s phone. Each one was cheerful, thoughtful, non-clingy. He is genuinely surprised that Adam has not returned any of them. This time, hearing the inevitable recording, Alec leaves just his name and his number. Leaving his office he encounters Sandra, who is walking down the corridor in a manner which cannot be described other than as skulking. She seems to be attempting to blend in with the wallpaper, like a human chameleon.

'Sandra?' says Alec mildly and he is taken aback by her abrupt turning to face him and the haunted, hunted look on her usually blank face, now suffused with tics and twitches.

'Sorry. Have you seen Rochelle?'

'No! Why should I? She's not my PA. I don't have that sort of relationship with her!'

Alec reminds himself that there is something singular going on and not to pay it too much attention so as not to encourage it.

'Yes, quite. It's just that I asked her to ask you to see me, so if you now see her can you tell her we have seen each other and she doesn't need to tell you.'

Sandra attempts to follow this although her frenzied state makes information coming in almost impossible to absorb. After a moment she nods.

'What was it you wanted to ask me?' she asks.

'Oh, something tiny. I've forgotten' says Alec, realising with a twinge of sadness that his statement is true. He is forgetting things. He's more aware of it this financial year than he was last year. Sometimes he puts it down to residual grief over his wife's death yet with another twinge he realises he hasn't thought about Alison for some time. Not, actually, since Blythe Hall. The forgetting, he concludes, is a sign of ageing. He is ageing and he hasn't made any further progress towards discovering who he is and finding a new mate to share the rest of his life with.

All this is going through Alec's mind and he suddenly comes back to reality with a start. Sandra is staring at him.

'Was there anything else?' she asks in a tone that clearly hopes the answer is in the negative.

'Oh, no, don't think so' says Alec, retiring in confusion. His mind continues to race. A couple of days ago he felt enormously content about Adam. Now Adam seems to be avoiding him and he has no idea why.

He resolves that as soon as he can leave the office he will go round to Adam's home. Perhaps the dear young man is sick?

A few hours later, bearing a bunch of flowers bought expensively *en route* from a Soho newsagent and already losing their bloom, Alec soberly rings Adam's doorbell. There is a flurry of movement from inside but the door is not opened. Alec frowns and rings again. He would normally be the most ineffectual of visitors, taking silence from the other side as a rebuke. Yet he is concerned, so he rings again, and also bangs on the door. After a tense moment the door is flung open and Alec recognises not Adam, but Darryl. Which, he thinks, makes sense since Darryl is Adam's flatmate.

'What?' snarls Darryl.

'Darryl, hello. It's me, Alec. Is Adam at home?'

Alarmingly, rather than responding in a like, polite, tone, Darryl throws his hands into the air, he pulls at his hair and even tries to tear off his shirt.

'How could Zac/Adam be at home! He's in Intensive Care!'

Alec processes this with a mixture of relief that he has not been forgotten, and horror that Adam is in a serious state.

'What happened?'

Darryl is also wrestling with mixed emotions. On the one hand from the depths of his distress over Adam he wants to tear the world apart and since Alec is braying stupid questions he feels an overwhelming urge to start with him. On the other hand he is on his way to the hospital and a taxi ride would ease the journey.

'Come!' he booms, grasping Alec with a manicured hand, the acrylic fingernails of which he has painted deepest and most tragic ebony.

In the taxi Darryl thumps the padded sides in a futile gesture to get the traffic moving faster. He glances sideways at Alec, who has been silent the whole way. If Alec were playing charades, the clue being a one-word film starring Kathy Bates, he would have no hesitation in answering 'Misery'. The lines in Alec's face are deeply etched with distress. Against his better judgment Darryl feels moved. He leans over and pats Alec's hand. Alec responds with a shudder and stares at him.

'At least he's not in Guy's situation.'

'Guy?'

'Yeah. His date. Didn't make the downhill run at all.'

Alec considers that Guy is a fairly unusual name, and that his therapist is called Guy, but dismisses it as a coincidence.

'I can see you're totally cut up' says Darryl.

Tears appear in Alec's world-weary eyes. 'He's my adopted grandson.'

Hearing this pound signs appear in Darryl's eyes as he calculates whether, as Zac's roommate and closest friend, he may be in for some windfall. In grief people are often financially reckless. Just ask a mortician.

'You poor dear' he whispers and gives Alec's hand another pat.

Some time is lost at the hospital because Darryl insists on their making their way to the ICU, whereas since Adam has only broken his leg he's recovering in a normal ward. Now they stand at the side of his bed. The patient has been sedated. Alec stretches out a tender hand to stroke his matted hair. Darryl wonders if the time is right to ask Alec if he can lend him some money just till the end of the month. A doctor, wearing a white coat and an intensely serious expression, approaches.

'I'm Mr White' he says solemnly. 'This is a sad business. Can I see you in my office?'

Seated in White's office, a comfortable room with internal glass windows, sited next to the ICU unit, Alec sips on a welcome hot tea while Darryl chews his way through a sandwich provided, although they don't know it, by the staff canteen.

'I'm afraid he's suffering from the trauma of the fall. His boyfriend was killed instantly, you know. And there are several breaks in the leg. It's not going to be easy.'

'What won't?' asks Darryl, genteelly wiping mayo.

White looks at him in minor confusion. 'Recovery.'

'Right' says Darryl. But he'll still live won't he?'

'Oh yes. However there will be enormous trauma, emotional devastation. He's only a young man, he had his whole life in front of him.'

At this Alec releases a pent-up sob.

Darryl leans forward confidentially and pats White's hand. 'Actually, if you knew that girl the way I do you'd know she's packed a *lot* of living into her earth years. And I'm proud she did. It's almost like she knew.'

White contemplates Darryl. Darryl uses an acrylic nail to remove a piece of cress wedged between two teeth. He sees White is looking at him strangely and wonders if White is interested so he gives him back a flirty look. He is not unmindful of the generous access doctors have to prescription drugs. And how Darryl is willing to be a guinea pig for any kind of new experiment involving psychedelics. White frowns.

'We can keep him here for the next ten days but beds, of course, are always in high demand. Which of you is going to look after him on his discharge?'

Alec and Darryl regard each other with great dismay.

'Thing is, Doc,' Darryl begins, 'I've been staying with Zac in his studio apartment. Turns out it's an illegal sublet and the legal tenant, a dancer who's been on a six- month cruise booking, is returning in two weeks. At which point I will be homeless so even though I loves my Zac, no can do.'

White wasn't crossing his fingers re Darryl. He turns with more hope to Alec. Aroused from a deep internal debate Alec leaves a silence before answering.

'Mr White. When I said I was Zac or rather Adam's grandfather I was speaking in a metaphorical sense. I hardly know the young man.'

'But' says Darryl, outraged that Alec is attempting to slide out of his responsibilities, 'you're the only man I know who's got any money or stability. Which is what our boy needs!'

Alec nods. 'Yes, and I am willing to use some of that money to pay for some sort of professional support for Zac/Adam. What I cannot, and I stress cannot, do, is take emotional responsibility for him. You see, not that you care or that it's any of your business, I have recently buried my wife. For many, many years, firstly due to oppressive violence and intimidation from my father, and then for the last thirty years because of the presence of my wife, I have never been myself. In the last few weeks I have begun to explore a different way of living, and to be a different person. I can tell you, not that you care or it's any of your business, that for the first time in my life I am beginning to understand and experience some degree of happiness. Freedom. Personal independence. I am not a young man. I have no idea how many or more likely how few years I have left. But I can assure you that I am prepared to fight to protect my few happy years left to me. And even though I ache for poor Adam, I must be resolute when I tell you that I am in no way able to personally look after him or bring him into my home environment. It's just too much.'

White is silent after this, as though impressed with Alec's passion. Then he speaks. 'Well, that's selfish. But understandable. So we have a situation where a patient has but two people who could help him and neither is in a position to do so. Such is modern life. If you're going to take a hammer to the nuclear family there are going to be examples of people thrown on the mercy of the professionals. However, Mr Bland, I did hear that you are willing to offer some sort of financial aid. That will certainly make Zac's living arrangements more comfortable. And, Darryl, I would hope that when your own living arrangements are sorted out you will find time to visit your friend.'

In the taxi returning to Soho both Alec and Darryl have been silent. Then Darryl turns to Alec. 'Is it just me or do you think he had a problem with us?'

Alec turns to Darryl and Darryl sees that his eyes are two little pools of distress. 'I can't believe I said what I did. Yet I honestly cannot change a syllable of what I said. I have never known a day's peace where I was able to do exactly what I wanted. Not in my entire life.'

'I know' says Darryl, attempting to staunch what he senses is about to become a river of sentiment.

'I don't have long. I don't have much hope. But if I am going to meet a man and form a permanent relationship, I cannot do it while I'm simultaneously caring for an invalid. I need to be able to go out for the night, or spontaneously jump on a plane for a week's holiday.'

'Got you' says Darryl, wondering if he should jump out at the next light.

Alec continues relentlessly. 'I've never thought about *me*. I want what I believe is called 'me time'.'

Darryl knows that the second 'me time' is introduced into the conversation that it's the beginning rather than the end of an unwelcome personal sharing. The taxi comes to a halt and Darryl asks to be let out. The driver releases the door and Darryl jumps out, shouting a quick goodbye to Alec over his shoulder. It's only as the taxi purrs its way away that Darryl remembers he neglected to put the financial bite on Alec. At least, he consoles himself as he completes on foot his return to Soho and Zac's temporary home, I don't have to hear any more of that crap.

Sixteen. SANDRA and DENNIS

'The trouble with you, Sandra' says her best friend, Abi Goodall, with the relaxed confidence of a woman who has been with her own woman for many years, 'is you like complications. Look at Jane and me. Both career women. Both under pressure. But she's my wife and we're happy. Because we're not trying to fight any big battles or show a false face to the world.'

'It's different for you' answers Sandra. For the last two hours she has been curled up on Abi and Jane's couch, weeping. 'I absolutely cannot bear that label at work.'

'But everyone has some sort of label. How do you think they label you now?'

Sandra looks over in genuine surprise. 'They don't label me at all.'

Abi and Jane burst into a peal of merry laughter. It goes on a little too long.

'Hon' says Abi, regarding her first ex with genuine affection, 'let me guess your current label.'

'Uptight spinster' offers Jane.

'Neurotic manhater' suggests Abi.

'Divorced shrew' says Jane.

'Manipulative climber' hazards Abi.

Sandra frowns. 'Are these just generic or are you working from what I've told you in the past?'

'Both. You are a woman, a powerful woman, and therefore you have a work label. So why don't you make it one that gives you benefits?'

'But! I don't know if Rochelle is gay. I've replayed and replayed that instant when I kissed her. Was there any pressure from her? Did she open her mouth at all? Did I get the feeling she liked it? I just don't know.'

'So invite her for another drink' suggests Jane. 'That's how this one got me.'

The two women exchange a look of great fondness. Sandra's mouth twists in annoyance. 'But you already knew about her. You knew she'd welcome the approach.'

'So' says Abi, remembering at precisely the right time something she read in a magazine recently, 'don't look at her. Look at who she looks at.'

'You mean I should hang around her and see if she unconsciously looks at men or women?'

'Got it.'

'But how am I going to hang around her if she shrinks and hides when she sees me?

'Not our problem.'

As life works out, the very next day an opportunity arises. A memo has been going round the office explaining that on Wednesday 14th a group of young graduates are being shown around the offices of Bland & Co. The idea is to give them a snapshot of an actual professional office environment. Sandra manages to move a couple of meetings and is on alert and hovering in the space outside Rochelle's cubical when the corridor is flooded with a colourful and also very physically attractive group of young people. Handsome men in suits, pretty women in dresses or smart jackets and trousers, bursting with youth and sexual allure.

It takes Sandra, in her position of wallflower, a little time to work out how the process works. First you have to look where Rochelle is looking, then you have to make sure that when you do you're looking at the same person. Rochelle, Sandra is pleased to note, is staring unashamedly at the group as the head of HR points out various items of interest. Yes, for a momentary flash Sandra is pretty sure Rochelle is looking at a sexy young redhead. But then everyone looks at redheads. Sandra's neck is becoming strained, reacting to the rapid swivelling action of attempting to match look with lookee. Sandra frowns as Rochelle appears to catch the eye of a strikingly attractive man of colour. If that's Rochelle's bag, Sandra thinks, I might as well go home now.

The group moves on. Sandra is a little slow to realise this and is left looking at Rochelle as the corridor empties. Rochelle's eyes are bright and her cheeks are becomingly flushed.

'That was charming' she says to Sandra.

This is the first time they have spoken in some days and it makes Sandra nervous.

'Oh?' she snaps. 'I thought they were boring. Very boring. I don't see what anyone sees in the young. Vastly over-valued.'

Rochelle's chatty manner changes like a tortoise withdrawing into its shell.

'Only trying to encourage' she mutters, turning to her files and away from Sandra.

Sandra continues to occupy a space on the wall, shifting her weight uneasily between her feet. After dealing with some enquiry Rochelle turns back. She regards Sandra coolly.

'Something to say, Sandra?'

'What's happening with Alec?' This is not the question Sandra wished to ask, but it's the best she could improvise. To her relief Rochelle responds warmly.

'I know. Have you noticed it too? I think he must be really missing his late wife.'

'Yes' says Sandra. Now that she's got Rochelle's unguarded attention she desperately desires to continue to hold it. 'I heard him crying in the men's toilet yesterday.'

This, she observes, is quite true although at the time she dismissed it. She's pleased to see how this goes over big. Rochelle's eyes widen into circles of compassion and concern.

'Oh *no!*'

'Yes. And I think I heard him on the phone the day before. Making … well it seemed like arrangements for some sort of nursing home. Do you think he's retiring?'

At the thought of her beloved Chairman leaving the company Rochelle's eyes fill with tender tears. Sandra's heart executes a high kick and she wonders if she should cross the distance that lies between them and crush Rochelle to her welcoming bosom. How would that play?

'Oh' she says hastily, 'I got the impression it was for someone else. But he's definitely not himself.'

'Do you think we should do something?' asks Rochelle and Sandra's heart begins a gavotte. A plan is formulating.

'I don't think we should do nothing' she replies cleverly. 'Why don't we discuss it further in the wine bar after work?'

And just like that, without seeming to have done so, Sandra has asked Rochelle out on a second date.

Meanwhile, as is always true in life, other narratives are unfolding. Dennis arrives for his regular cleaning session cum extra humiliation with Jerry. Jerry takes time to answer and Dennis's usual vague demenour of irritation increases. Jerry finally throws the door open, regards Dennis with disgust, and turns back into the flat without even a civil greeting. Which is appropriate behaviour from a sex pig. Dennis brightens.

Sometime later Dennis has turned the bathroom into showroom perfection and has also restored the kitchen into a space where you can actually see and access the counter tops. During this transformation Jerry has been wondering what Dennis can do next. Although it doesn't easily show, Jerry takes his position as a dirty pig seriously. Yes, he never wipes his behind properly and of course he wears the same underpants for a month, that's child's play, yet he knows competition for the fetish pound is keen. A disappointing visit means one fewer regular. During the week just past, however, he had a few old chums round for a pizza cum orgy and the stink from his bedroom has to be smelt to be fully believed.

'You're needed in there' he says, throwing a dismissive thumb in the direction of the bedroom. To his surprise Dennis doesn't immediately proceed to go but stands as though there's something on his mind.

'What?' grunts Jerry. He becomes a little intimidated as Dennis doesn't reply, instead Dennis regards Jerry with what his mother would call 'an old-fashioned look'.

'Nothing' says Dennis but he says it with a frisson. A few seconds later, to Jerry's relief, Dennis proceeds into the bedroom. Jerry watches as Dennis reels in response to the hell it contains.

'What the fuck has been going on?' Dennis thunders.

Jerry is now truly confused. He rallies, thrusting his hand down his own shorts. 'You want some of this in there?' he snarls, but with less confidence than usual.

'Actually, mate' says Dennis carefully, 'I do believe I'd sooner stick my head down your toilet.'

'Fine' says Jerry, 'but don't blame me if it's all clean and scrubbed from your visit.'

'You imbecile' shouts Dennis. 'Can't you read the signs? Can't you interpret body language?'

Jerry thinks and has to agree he cannot. 'What's up, bro?' he says in a new and humble voice.

Dennis strides out of the bedroom, slamming the door. 'I suggest you instruct professional cleaners to restore that room to a degree suitable for human occupation!'

Confused to an extreme degree, Jerry follows Dennis into the kitchen. Dennis, even without his master's consent, has poured himself a glass of water and now stands by the clean sink, drinking it.

'Dennis. Babe. What's the matter?'

This simple appeal causes Dennis's stern manner to entirely crumble. His legs begin to shake and his chin trembles. Tears gush from his eyes like two fully-opened taps. Jerry rushes across to him and grasps him in his manly, tattooed arms.

'Darling! You know it's just play. You know I'd never want to upset you!'

At any other time, hearing that his master is capable of such soppy talk would cause Dennis to quit his flat at high speed. Right now he can only cuddle into Jerry's whiffy yet comforting embrace.

'Oh Jerry' he wails. 'I went to the world's worst party last week!'

'You tell me all about it' coos Jerry sweetly.

'My PA, Philip, had a birthday. It was in this loft and these guys were leaning against the wall. But it wasn't a wall. Some fuckwit had covered a fucking great void with a canvas blind and they leaned against it and they. They fell! And one of them was killed outright and the other is in hospital.'

'Oh dearest' whispers Jerry, kissing Dennis's heaving cheeks tenderly, 'and were they close friends of yours?'

'No' says Dennis. 'But it was a horrible sight. And ever since then … Listen, Jerry, do you mind if you don't humiliate me tonight? I'm feeling pretty messed up. Can't we just do something relaxing?'

'You mean I could mummify you?' asks Jerry.

'No! I mean we could order takeaway and watch a box set.'

While Dennis is washing his face in the bathroom Jerry, from idle curiosity, does a search for 'two men in loft party fall'. When Dennis returns, feeling a little more composed, he's surprised to find Jerry in tears.

'Oh Jerry, you don't have to be upset for me.'

'Piss off you twat' says Jerry but not vindictively. 'I knew one of the guys. The one in hospital. Sweet kid.'

'Oh really?' says Dennis in a cool tone. 'How well do you know him?'

'Dennis come on! Can you be jealous of someone who's in hospital?'

Dennis considers this and nods affirmatively. A damaged and insecure childhood stays with you. 'Still, I'm probably more upset than you because I actually saw it happening.'

'Yeah, but Zac was in love with me. You didn't know that did you?'

Too late Jerry discovers that Dennis is too frail to play one-upmanship. Dennis pulls away, produces his wallet from which he pulls a clutch of banknotes, throws the notes at Jerry and storms out.

'Fine. Go. Good riddance!' cries Jerry.

It's only once he's tucking into takeaway and enjoying the latest costume drama that Jerry reflects that for the last week he's been counting the days till Dennis would sort out the mess in his bedroom. Whereas he's made a fine reputation as a sex pig he's starting to appreciate the benefits of not waking up in what smells like Satan's jockstrap.

'Damn you Dennis' he shouts. 'Damn you Zac' he continues. He becomes aware of the thick silence. Since his unwelcome guest moved on the silence has been gathering in layers. 'Damn you Darryl' he concludes. He could use a punter calling right now. Take his mind off the evening so far, and also make him some money. Yet no shrill ringing interrupts the increasing silence. What if all the kinks were at that disastrous party? He knows this thought is merely rampant paranoia, yet it chimes in so perfectly with his gloom that he can't dismiss it. Every now and then the sound of silence increases in intensity. Jerry whimpers and turns up the telly a little louder. He concentrates on worrying about what Lady Claudia is going to do about her unrequited love for Lord Spencer. He's aware it's not really distracting him.

Seventeen. ALEC

Standing around, waiting for something to happen, I'm aware that I've successfully avoided Golders Green crematorium for years and now I've been here twice in the last two months. Of course, the first was much more intensely meaningful, being to do with my late wife Alison. I am here principally because Adam, from his hospital sick bed, begged me to attend the service in his name. What I haven't told him is that I also have a personal reason to be here, seeing that Guy was my therapist. Looking around I believe I can spot Guy's other clients. They're a mixed bag and their reactions to his shocking demise are also mixed. Some stand silent, looking downwards, not wanting to be part of the gathering.

A couple of others appear to be family, at least if the muttered discussion about who is going to get what from Guy's will is an indicator. There's one young lad in a continual stream of tears. I don't know why I'm drawn to his display of grief since I habitually avoid open sentiment, yet I feel drawn to comfort him.

'Hello. I'm Alec. Did you know Guy well?'

The young man turns blue, tragic, eyes in my direction. 'He was my lover, my best friend, my guide, my confidant, my universe!'

'Oh' I say, somewhat intimidated by the litany, 'so you knew him well?'

'If only he'd stayed faithful to me' says the other with bitterness, 'and not tried to see what else was out there. What was out there was disaster!'

'True' I can but agree. 'Would you like to have a cup of coffee or something? When this thing is over? My name's Alec by the way.'

The young man looks at me strangely. ‘So. This is a day of firsts. I’ve never been cruised at the cremation of the love of my life before.’

‘No’ I reply thoughtfully, ‘mind you I didn’t know all that other stuff. I just thought you looked like you could use a coffee.’

At this the young man leans on my shoulder and weeps loudly. I’m not, as I’ve already noted, good with overt signs of sentiment. Yet no one seems put out by it and there’s something disarming about youth and beauty trustingly weeping on one.

The service goes as well as any of these ceremonies can be expected to. People one doesn’t know stand and say how much they are going to miss the person. People who aren’t poets read poems they scribbled down at three in the morning. Other people weep brokenly from the front stalls. It’s like viewing a long running TV series where everyone else knows what’s going on but one was merely flicking channels and is now stuck. Of course, Guy was my therapist but I must confess I didn’t know his private life was so racy.

It’s a coincidence that Guy was so fatally acquainted with my Adam. People sometimes tell me that they don’t believe in coincidence. I find that puzzling. Coincidence isn’t like the reality of Father Christmas, or ghosts. You don’t have to believe. Sometimes, though, life’s coincidences astound me.

If my wife hadn’t died I wouldn’t have gone to therapy and encountered Guy. If I hadn’t gone to Blythe Hall I wouldn’t have met Adam. If Guy hadn’t been leaving his partner he wouldn’t have met Adam. If Adam’s friend Philip hadn’t had a loft party at which some mental defective had rigged a death trap none of us would be here and Adam wouldn’t be sunk deep in despair and plaster.

As I’m looking round I spot what appears to be another coincidence.

'Hello Philip' I say, joining him where he stands with a couple of other young men. 'I hadn't realised you and Adam's friend Philip are one.'

'Oh' says Philip. 'Adam's my best friend. You probably know him as Zac?'

'Actually I know him as Adam. We met at Blythe Hall. Why would you expect me to know him as Zac?'

I recognise Philip, of course, since he is Dennis's PA from work.

'Oh, nothing. I'm here because I was at the hospital and Adam begged me to come here in his name.'

'There's a coincidence' I reply. 'He said something on the same lines to me.'

Philip's face is working and I can tell he's going to speak more. Then I feel a hand tucking itself into my arm and I turn to see that the weeping young man has returned.

'I'm sorry but I can't face going in there alone' he explains. 'Could you go in with me?'

'Of course but don't you have other friends here?'

'I've been talking to them' says the young man grimly, 'and seems everyone thinks Guy was fantastic and I was just using him.'

'Oh dear' I respond. 'Of course I'll sit with you. This is Philip. We work together.'

'Thanks. Hi. I'm Ted.'

Afterwards coffee turns into lunch. Ted expresses an urgent need for alcohol so we adjourn to the pub two doors away. A quiet refuge, it seems. Ted has a lot to say. I can boil it down to his being very angry about Guy, and that he's feeling humiliated both by Guy having died in the company of another man, and also because Ted, in his quest to find a Guy replacement, has been hitting the streets of shame.

'This one guy, he sounded good on the phone. I didn't mind him being in his 80s, I like a mature man. Guy was 50 and I sometimes used to think he was too young for me. Not yet settled down, you know? This guy, Cedric, insisted on bringing his nurse on the date. And she wasn't one of those discreet nurses whispering about, doing good and keeping their mouths shut. She was from the Caribbean and everything Cedric or I said reminded her of something that happened to a relative or a friend back in the old country.'

I laugh. Ted smiles. I've sometimes been aware that people like it when you laugh at something they've said.

'So I've now made a rule. No one over 75.'

I cough. 'You wouldn't think it' I say, 'but I'm 71.'

'Oh great' says Ted. 'Actually I didn't like to ask. Originally I had decided 70 but having met you I thought I'd better move the line up a bit.'

I'm not sure this is flattering. I think it sounds more like harsh reality. Yet staring at Ted I'm also aware that he's not the slightest bit discomforted by the age gap.

'Age makes no difference' he says as though reading my mind.

'That's good to hear' I respond and silently make a note of this helpful phrase for future repetition.

'So you like me and I like you' says Ted.

'But. Haven't we just come from the cremation of your life's great love?'

'Oh yeah. I mean I'm still messed up. If there's one thing I've taken from Guy's death it's that we don't have the luxury of pissing about. I mean, especially with someone like you. If I don't get in there immediately who knows what might thwart me.'

'You mean some other dashing young man might carry me off?' I ask jocularly.

'I was thinking more you could drop dead of a heart attack' he responds.

I frown.

'Very complimentary. However, as you've said, you are messed up inside. I feel sad that I could be the man for you, but you're not ready.'

'Oh yeah' says Ted. 'But I always do the same thing when I start a relationship.'

'Light a candle for good luck?'

Ted laughs. 'Naah. Book into a weekend with the new man at Blythe Hall. There's no better atmosphere for deciding whether or not to go forward with a new relationship.'

Blythe Hall? I think. There's a coincidence.

Fortunately Blythe has an immediate, double room cancellation. Something about the two men couldn't decide who was going to sleep on which side of the bed so instead they've broken up. I solemnly read the long numbers on my credit card over the phone and on Friday night I am again standing in the august and exciting hallway of Blythe.

'You won't believe it' I say to Ted, 'but I was in the exact same place only a few weeks ago.'

'Who did you come with?' asks Ted with immediate suspicion. I laugh jocularly and his glare increases. Hastily I explain that I was a virgin, that I came here not knowing my arse from my elbow. Or anyone else's for that matter. I decline to add that this is where I met Adam. I'm getting the feeling that after Guy's treatment of him Ted is feeling vulnerable. And defensively aggressive, if I'm using the term correctly.

Andrew is once again leading the weekend. Once again there is a cornucopia of delightful men in residence. I'm not exactly sure what Ted thinks we will gain from the weekend yet I'm feeling light-headed and light-hearted and I'm learning to let go and not worry about things before they happen.

The opening address goes well and there are no problems during the cocktail meet and greet. Dinner is edible and plentiful and Ted's smuggled a bottle of Scotch in our suitcase so we're neither of us sober. As we walk along the corridor I can hear the happy splashes of group bathing. I turn with a chuckle to Ted. On his face is a look of thunder. I feel intimidated and I don't comment on it. Perhaps he was here with Guy at some point and it's bringing back tender memories.

After dinner Ted and I walk in the spacious, well-tended grounds. Ted holds my hand throughout. When we are the furthest from the house we turn to face it.

'Look at that' I say. 'Here we are in the black country night. All around us is stillness and emptiness. Yet right there is a great hive of light and colour and energy.'

'I don't know about that shit' responds Ted. 'I sell life insurance.'

I'm at a loss for how to reply. Turns out I don't need to because Ted throws himself into my arms and thrusts his tongue into my mouth. Thank heavens for regular flossing.

After a night of unbridled passion I feel as I have never felt before. Ted is bizarrely besotted with me. He glares at anyone who comes to sit at our table. Eventually we are joined by Andrew, who isn't put off by Ted's display of temperament. Perhaps it's even a display of ownership. The idea of belonging to such an attractive, youthful partner fills me with radiant happiness and wonder. The only sad aspect in my horizon is the equally delightful young man currently languishing in hospital. Before coming out to Blythe I paid one of my frequent visits to dear Adam. I told him where I was coming and he turned his head away. I could see his eyes filling with tears. I could have kicked myself for my insensitivity.

'So how long have you two known each other?' asks Andrew.

'We met at my ex's cremation' Ted explains.

'Cool. When was that?'

'Two days ago.'

If Andrew thinks this is a rebound situation he's too polite and sensitive to say. He nods, smiles and begins to move away.

'I look forward to working with you tomorrow' I say to his departing back and Andrew stops.

'Oh?' asks Ted in a suspicious tone.

This is the secret agenda I have been holding, my other reason for coming to Blythe. And I'm not going to let Ted being silly spoil it. This weekend doesn't have the same timetable as the first one, it's more informal, you have to ask if you want to experience any of Blyth's particular attractions.

'Yes.' I turn to Ted and smile. 'Darling, I'm going to participate in the nude encounter!'

'But why?' snarls Ted, 'they'll only point at you and make fun of you.'

'Now wait' says Andrew. 'That's exactly what's not going to happen. The nude encounter is a tasteful, positive, supportive experience. I've rarely seen it go wrong.'

'Rarely isn't never' snaps Ted. 'I forbid you to.'

I exchange a frustrated look with Andrew.

'Darling. I am an adult, heaven knows. And I'm capable of taking responsibility for myself. I am fully prepared to be laughed at. Yet at the same time, you must appreciate that I have never been nude in front of a group of men. I honestly feel that in order to fully be a gay man I have to put myself through the experience. At least once. So book me a place, thanks' I say to Andrew. He nods and walks away. Ted turns hot, angry eyes and stares into mine.

'You're going to hate it. They'll make fun of you. They're just a bunch of prissy queens.'

I nod. 'You're probably right. It's exactly the worst nightmare scenario for me. Yet that's why I really have to do it. I hope you'll join in too.'

A smirk appears on Ted's usually innocent face. 'Okay, Alec. I'll do just that.'

We are a group of about 12, meeting in the Joan Collins room. Outside, singles and couples stroll the lawns, enjoying a moment's respite. Inside we are discreetly removing our outer garments and placing them in a neat pile, down the side wall, as instructed. I have been hoping that someone I met last time would be here and I think yearningly of Donny, so I wouldn't feel as though I was launching myself into an entirely alien world. However, that is the situation. It adds another layer of inner doubt to my being here in the first place. Clearly Ted is correct. I look around furtively and I don't like the look on these men's faces. They seem far too ready to criticise any physical faults, and I am not so dazzled by my overnight passion with Ted to be fooled into thinking I have regained my rugby days slimness.

A very thin youth in his mid-twenties goes first. The group admires his height, the whiteness of his skin, his excellent teeth and his narrow hips. He seems well satisfied. Then a man about 40, shorter, wider, hairier. The group has to work a little harder in this instance, yet kind appreciation is given to his broadness, funkiness, sexiness, daddiness and hairiness. The man swaggers back to his spot. Ted smiles at me as though daring me to put myself up next. I hesitate. Next is a man in his thirties, balding, very ordinary, the sort of man you wouldn't notice if you were alone with him in a lift. He is complimented on his straight-acting looks, his elegant profile, the attractive shape of his head and his muscular legs. As he sits I glance at Ted, wanting to reassure him that surely I will be fine. There's a silence. Here goes. I stand up and shuffle forward through the pile of bodies to the observation space.

I am suddenly on automatic, mimicking what the others have done. I turn sideways, I turn around and back. I bend over. I realise with a terrible jolt of reality that I am by far the oldest person in the room. I have not only the years of life on me, but the years of neglect. When you have lived an aesthetic existence for several decades, by which I more truthfully mean existing in celibacy and loneliness, eating and drinking are one's principal comforts. Being known as a loveable old walrus is acceptable in the corridors of business because no one is inviting you to strip. Standing in front of a group of men of middling to genuine beauty in appearance is a very, very different scenario. Which I have understood far too late. Sweat begins to pour. I have thrust myself into the mouth of the lion and it's ready to bite my head off.

'I love your balls' says a friendly voice.

'Oh yeah' responds another. 'I mean those babies are the size of oranges.'

'Yeah' a third joins in. 'But look at those nipples. I mean they're hard, they're sticking out an inch. I know this is only about appreciation, but I want those babies in my mouth!'

Andrew has to bring the gathering to order, reminding them that we are here to be supportive, not slutty.

'I never had a thing for old guys until now' says a new voice. 'Now I get it.'

'Can he bend over again' asks the first man. 'I didn't get the whole picture.'

'No he can't' responds Andrew. 'Anything else?'

'His skin is much more supple than I thought it would be. And naked his face makes more sense. It's like …'

I frown. I'm about to be labelled a walrus.

'It's like I would imagine Burt Reynolds looks now. You can tell he used to be dead sexy.'

Andrew brings my viewing to a close and I weave my way back to where Ted is waiting. On the way a couple of appreciative hands stroke my legs. I regain my place and smile at Ted. 'That wasn't too bad' I say and inside I celebrate a triumph. I have survived my worst nightmare and got some validation in the process. Ted says nothing. He also declines to present himself to the group which I did not realise was allowed.

'But darling' I say with feeling, 'you have a lovely body. Why not be celebrated for it?'

'I'm not in the mood' he explains, grinding the words out singly.

A little while later we are enjoying tea on the lawn when Ted tells me he needs to make a phone call. This entails retrieving his phone from our room. After he has left me I regards the lawns and trees with great pleasure. This weekend I have consummated my new identity as a gay man and had my aged body complimented. All is wonderful and I cannot imagine anything will go awry.

One of the men from the nude encounter drops into the seat opposite me.

'Hello Alec. Where's your boyfriend?'

'Oh he's gone off to make a phone call.'

'If he's anything like my ex he's going to be about an hour.'

'Do you think so?' I enquire plaintively.

'Oh yeah, he'll have a mass of messages and he'll get caught up. You can forget seeing him till dinner.'

'Oh dear' I reply in some confusion. 'I don't know what I'm going to do. It's funny but in this place one feels the need for constant activity and stimulation.'

'You could join us' says the man diffidently.

'Oh, that sounds splendid. What are you doing? Walking? Playing cards?'

It turns out that what he and a couple of his friends are doing is participating in the other special attraction of Blythe Hall: the shared bath.

I had been looking forward to bathing with Ted later. Yet if he's not going to be around till dinner, and if afterwards I'm going to feel too tired to bathe, I suppose it's only practical to have a bath now. Of course, baths are usually a singular affair. However we are at Blythe and I feel very secure in my new relationship. Since I will be bathing with the same group of men who were so kind about me earlier, how could Ted object? I'll simply explain I wanted to be pink and scrubbed for our night of passion to come.

The baths at Blythe are no bigger than those in other parts of the country. One quickly learns to be very careful with water because the multiple immersions cause the water to slop over the side. Although a newcomer to this event I discover that if I sit on the end and immerse only my lower half, I can enjoy the warm water while ensuring the floor remains dry.

'Here I come!' cries the particularly thin, tall young man. The next instant he slaps a hand full of soap suds in my crotch. I pull back in surprise. 'I've been wanting to do this all afternoon!' he cries. Really the feeling is so warm, so relaxing, I know I should explain that I am here with my new lover, yet the sheer unfamiliarity of the situation overwhelms me. Perhaps for these other bathers this is just another jape but for me this comes like a deep revelation after many years of sad solitude.

It would appear that the thin young man is not alone in wanting to initiate me into the mysteries of the group bath. Other hands approach and I'm ready to accept that I have died and gone to a particularly generous heaven when the door is thrown open. There stands Ted, phone in hand, fury on face.

'What the fuck!' he shouts. 'I turn my back for one moment and you're having sex with a bunch of randy braindead queens!'

'Watch it mate' says one. 'I'm a Church of England vicar.'

'And I'm a policeman recently commended for outstanding bravery' says another.

'You and I. Are finished!' howls Ted.

'But darling,' I splutter. 'It's just a harmless bath together. I've never done anything like this before. Don't spoil it for me.'

'We are over!' howls Ted.

With dignity I remove the hands still attached to me. 'Darling, think. You wanted to see how we would get on this weekend. I'm still your man. You're still the one for me.'

'I don't want you anymore' responds Ted. 'I thought you were different. I thought you were loyal.'

'No' I say, stepping fully out and wrapping myself wet in my bathing robe. 'You thought I didn't have a choice. You thought I was desperate.'

Although he's too angry to reply this seems to pierce through Ted's anger and strike at the heart of his thinking.

'Fine' Ted replies. 'Okay, I thought that after Guy if I went for an old bloke I'd feel more in control.'

'That's hardly flattering to me. Or kind' I reply.

'I told you I'm in a weird place' he responds.

The other three in the room have been exchanging glances and now the one who is apparently acting as foreman speaks up.

'Look guys, can you take the analysis elsewhere? We're trying to have a quiet bath.'

'Drop dead!' howls Ted. 'I'm packing and I'm moving!'

'But darling' I say, attempting to dampen down the rising distress I'm feeling. One moment I thought my future was mapped out yet now it's again in total flux.

'Darling, think. There's no transport available till the morning. Where will you sleep?'

'I'll sleep with Andrew' answers Ted snappily.

'Andrew!?'

'Who do you think found me in our room and told me what you were up to?'

I am about to question whether Andrew, as convenor of the weekend, should be interfering in the personal lives of individual participants when Ted turns on his heel and stomps off. I look to the other three and they make gestures encouraging me to return to the bath. I decline and with heavy heart I pad back to our room. Its emptiness rebukes me like a slap. Ted is nowhere to be seen unless, I presume, one looks in Andrew's room.

I finish drying, select a new outfit for the evening, and pad sadly along the corridor and downstairs.

'Having a good time?' asks someone with a buzzcut and tank top, around 30, I've not seen before.

'I honestly couldn't tell you' I respond. 'If this is what gay life is like, either I came in too late or I simply can't read and understand the instructions.'

'Whatever' the other responds. 'Want to join a game of strip poker?'

Eighteen. ROCHELLE

To begin to unravel the mystery that is Rochelle we need to look for evidence from her childhood home environment. Ordinary facts must be seen from another angle, so the little clues and commentaries she drops into conversation at work can be gathered and slid into the appropriate places. Only when we have all the pieces and stand back can we fathom her depths.

The sad fact is that until now no one has bothered. Rochelle and her support stockings were a one-day joke when she first became Alec's PA. After the sniggers had died down, the eyeballs had stopped rolling, everyone was content to label her the frustrated spinster and get on to divining more sexy mysteries, like whom the photocopier repair man who wears blue dungarees was keen on.

Rochelle was a quiet child at school, so diffident that if a teacher entered a room in which she was the sole pupil present the teacher would say in an aggrieved tone into the air 'Where are all the kids?'

During her 20s, once Rochelle had finished studying assiduously to become proficient in typing, shorthand and filing, guests would politely enquire if Rochelle had a young man. Rochelle's mother would answer for her. 'Why would Rochelle need a man? Here she has her own bedroom, her own bathroom, and all the freedom in the world!' Rochelle would not even raise her gentle eyes from her book. Once, for a lark, on her birthday, the girls in the office gave her a card that read on the outside 'Want to find the perfect man?' and on the inside 'Then get rid of your mother.' This horrified Rochelle, she thought her mystery had been cracked, her privacy invaded. She came out in an ugly strawberry rash and had to lie in bed for a week. Her mother put it around that she'd suffered a miscarriage. For no other reason than she was bored and wanted Rochelle, even in her distress, to provide her with some amusement.

When Rochelle was 32 her mother died. Oh, there was no evidence of foul play. She merely tripped on the top step and fell down the stairs. There was a little gossip in the village about the coincidence, since Rochelle's mother had been a huge Laura Ashley devotee, and Dame Laura died in the same tragic fashion. Then the loudest gossip stepped in, declaring that there was no such thing as coincidence and village life moved on. Although the house is worth almost a million pounds, and Rochelle takes nearly two hours each way to make the journey to work and then home, she has never considered selling the house. As her mother used to point out, she has her own rooms and plenty of space.

An almost unreadable clue to Rochelle lies in the single postcard she has pinned on the notice board on the wall next to her desk. It depicts one of Stanley Spencer's fascinating paintings of Cookham churchyard. Occasionally the more artistic of her colleagues will notice and ask Rochelle if she is a big fan of Spencer's. To their surprise the usually perfectly equable Rochelle will look up, eyes on fire, and snap 'I cannot stand the man!'

Yet she continues to retain the postcard. So we must posit that there is a connection between the card and Rochelle but it's not obvious. The answer lies in a brief examination of Spencer's love life. His relationship with his second wife, in fact. Spencer painted a voluptuous, sensuous, extraordinary portrait of himself and Patricia. The two are both obscenely, voluptuously nude, Patricia's body firm and inviting, Spencer crouching over her in an attitude of hopeless yearning. For Patricia was a Lesbian and the marriage was a disaster.

It isn't Rochelle who is a major Spencer buff. It was her mother. Their bookshelves are clogged with books devoted to his artwork and the various biographies in which he features. As a child the mother had once been introduced to Spencer and often, whether or not she was asked, would retell the story of this colourless brief encounter to Rochelle. Always with the story came the warning, like the wagging finger on the cigarette packet.

'Spencer was the greatest painter this country has ever produced! And he was destroyed, humiliated, castrated by Patricia! That is what Lesbians do!'

Rochelle never questioned her mother's take on the Spencer marriage so she never even considered that Spencer was a madman to marry someone who would never love him in the ordinary way.

There were a number of other ways in which Rochelle's mother had blunted and stunted a girl who began with a cheerful and pleasant attitude to the world. But the Spencer warning was the most pervasive. Hence the postcard, given to Rochelle when she started at Bland's, by her mother.

On the writing side did it say 'Darling, I'm rooting for you on your first day?' No. Did it say 'I've always believed in my wonderful baby?' No.

It said 'Lesbians are everywhere and they will destroy you. Beware.'

Had Rochelle been of steelier mettle she might have answered her mother saying that she didn't know what she was but when she worked it out, she would let her mother know. Instead, from that day to this, she has worked for Bland's under the daily watchful eye of her mother's craziest contribution to her damaged upbringing.

Thus Rochelle is looking forward to her rendezvous with Sandra with feelings both wildly for and against. More than once since the moment Sandra seized her in that terrifying, thrilling embrace she has replayed the seconds leading up to it. Questions keep unfolding and Rochelle trembles at their implication. Did she behave in such a way that Sandra has picked up some vibe from her? Is Sandra a predatory Lesbian of the kind her mother warned her about? Should Rochelle send an email crying off with some excuse and suggest that the two catch up in Sandra's office tomorrow? With others present?

This last has been the most attractive possibility, given that it means Rochelle can make her usual long journey home to an empty house. It's ultimately this rather than the fear of again meeting Sandra in intimate surroundings that prompts Rochelle to do nothing about the arrangement. Four times during the day she excuses herself, goes into the ladies, carefully checks that none of the stalls are occupied, looks in the mirror and recites to herself:

'It's nothing. Tonight I'm just going for a drink with Sandra. At some point we will have drunk so much Sandra won't hold back any longer. She will kiss me. We will get a taxi back to her place. And tomorrow I will be what I have always wanted to be. A professional Lesbian.'

Could it be that from early childhood Rochelle's mother had noticed something different in her child? It wasn't as though there were signs that are helpful in identifying other young gay girls: a liking for d-i-y and football, a passionate dislike of pink, dolls and any suggestion she will one day make a wonderful wife to a lucky man? In Rochelle's case her mother had so thoroughly crushed her delicate nature that there were no signs other than a liking for her own company and books and that could apply to just about any lonely child.

It is a great pity that Rochelle's mother, her own nature twisted by more than dark thoughts over Spencer's unfortunate marriage choice, didn't talk openly to Rochelle and encourage her to follow her own path as dictated by her inner preferences. But she didn't, then she fell downstairs and died so there's not much juice to be squeezed from that lemon. Instead we continue to regard Rochelle curiously. There have been a couple of incidents in the past, girls from work, women from the village or whom she met on the train, who seemed to be expressing interest in Rochelle. These she had fled. Will Sandra be able to change

Rochelle's appalling emotional record or will Sandra, in her eagerness to force the rose to open its petals, blow it? The buttons of Sandra's mind are difficult to undo and Sandra's fingers may be too blunt.

'Two Chablis?' asks Sandra, glancing at the waiter, smiling at Rochelle. 'And bring us some nuts and snacks.'

'You mean our festive basket?' asks the waiter.

'Does it contain nuts and snacks?'

'And olives.'

'Then why are you even asking me? Duuh' snaps Sandra. Rochelle is dismayed to hear that it sounds like Sandra is in a belligerent mood. At the office Rochelle has always avoided Sandra at these times, yet wedged round a tiny, uncomfortable table she has no wiggle room.

'So. Alec. What's happening with Alec' Sandra says in an efficient tone. Rochelle realises that Sandra is in an all-business mood. Perhaps she's made a terrible mistake. Perhaps Sandra always kisses people she's just had a drink with goodbye. Perhaps everything that Rochelle has both dreaded and deeply craved from Sandra is a huge joke, yet another way life has set her up to be laughed at.

'Alec's fine' she says politely, as he's told her to respond to queries in person or on the phone.

'What do you mean fine' snaps Sandra. 'Anyone with half a brain can see the man is literally falling apart. What do they teach you in secretarial college anyway?'

Sandra then leans back and slaps the table causing the flatware to jump and ping.

'Shorthand?' asks Rochelle in an unnaturally high voice, any flavour of control gained from those mirror pep talks fleeing like the night before the first rays of the glaring sun.

'What?' responds Sandra as though it is the world's official most stupid answer.

'I can't think when you intimidate me' responds Rochelle.

Sandra looks round, takes a deep breath, watches momentarily as other patrons of the restaurant dart to and froe. 'Why would I bloody intimidate you?' asks Sandra, a question she believes not inappropriate to the occasion. 'What the hell has this to do with you? I asked about bloody Alec.'

In order to interpret Sandra's foul mood we need learn only that Sandra hasn't slept properly the last two nights. She tried but thoughts about this meeting, this moment robbed her of sweet repose. Therefore, she's tired and irritated. In addition, just before she came out, she heard that a new venture she's spent much time and effort on has been awarded to another company. Still, she had reflected, at least I'm meeting Rochelle for a drink. It is only when she acknowledges that the Rochelle she had been looking forward to a quiet word with and the Rochelle in front of her seem to be two entirely different creatures that her really bad mood kicked in.

'I haven't seen much of a change' Rochelle ventures. She racks her brain to offer Sandra some morsel of intrigue that will satisfy her bloodlust for ammunition.

'He went to a cremation yesterday, and he's visiting the hospital again.'

'Who's in hospital?' asks Sandra quickly. In the past she has been in a situation where a work rival had a serious illness in the family and Sandra had been able to put someone else's misfortune to her advantage.

'I don't really know. It's a man. I mean that was what the card had to say. 'To Adam, from Alec.'

'You're sure that's all the card said?'

'To Adam, from Alec.'

'So this Adam, is he a relative? A nephew, cousin, uncle? What sort of man sends another man flowers in any case?'

'I'm sure I don't know' responds Rochelle, now in dank misery.

'What sort of flowers were they?' Sandra once received something from a man who very carefully explained that the reason why they weren't roses was so she wouldn't become confused that he fancied her. Then he handed her a cactus.

'What sort of flowers were they?'

'Just flowers. Red. Yellow.'

'Do I have to produce a nursery catalogue and flick through the pages until you spot the right one? Do you not understand that there is a secret language to flowers? The variety of flowers is as important as flowers at all!'

'I can't tell you' says Rochelle, verging on tears. 'Alec just told me to send a hundred pounds of flowers, in those colours, to that hospital.' Rochelle would desperately like to have further details. What Alec didn't explain to her is that yellow and red, in the proper order, are the colours of joy.

Sandra leans forward, her interest piqued. 'A hundred pounds? When I fractured my finger, the old miser contributed exactly two pounds to my get-well gift fund.'

'You think it's significant?'

'Significant in that there was only enough to buy me a bottle of Californian sparkling wine.'

'I mean, do you think the money value is significant?'

‘I really hadn’t realised how thick you are’ says Sandra belligerently.

Rochelle’s lip trembles. Sandra hisses in irritation and Rochelle stops trembling.

Then, as an afterthought, a tiny pearl of information that Rochelle, broken by Sandra’s attitude, doubts will be of interest, she adds ‘Today he got me to call his lawyer and then had a long conversation. I couldn’t make out all of it but it seemed to do with setting up some sort of a regular monthly payment. Of two thousand pounds.’

Sandra is so excited she swings her arm out and punches a passing waiter. The waiter protests but is ignored. ‘He’s being blackmailed!’

Rochelle is both happy to see that Sandra’s eyes are now shining and concerned that Sandra’s eyes have such a calculating gleam in them. Still, she reasons, if she can leave Sandra to plot she can still be at home and have a bath before she subsides into a weeping mess of disappointment.

‘Fine. We’re on a roll. Excellent. And of course you’ll keep me briefed? Any tiny development. Don’t censor, bring it to Mama.’

Rochelle has always been prized for not only her outstanding technical skills but also her quiet loyalty.

‘I’m not sure I can do that, Sandra. I mean, I met you this evening because I thought we were going to help Alec in his present grief. If Alec has got himself into trouble I’m not sure I am the person to help bring him down.’

The triumphant gleam abruptly fades from Sandra’s eyes and is replaced by a furious, baleful stare.

‘Oh?’ she says in a tone that could freeze-dry fresh spring vegetables, ‘So you’re not going to help me?’

‘Of course not. Why on earth would you think I would?’

The reply that hovers on Sandra's lips is 'Because, you little fool, I'm madly, passionately in love with you!' This exact phrase, in fact, she heard only the previous evening in a black and white 1940s war romance. That didn't end well either.

'Because I'm asking you to' she amends.

'But I don't want to' replies Rochelle. In her mind she is already boarding the train home.

'But …' says Sandra. And then she nods her head. After all the woman has a point. Banal and entirely unhelpful, but a point.

Then the snacks appear. Sandra was about to sweep off into the night but at the sight of food she remembers she hasn't eaten all day. Rochelle is also too polite to stomp off while there is food. So the two unhappily, silently, eat their way through the restaurant's festive basket.

As she's mopping the last of the olive oil with the final bread roll, the alcohol that has been such an unacknowledged influence on her, bringing out her darkest side, becomes balanced by the calories in the food. In an instant Sandra has a vision of the scene from an entirely new aspect. She's sitting after work opposite the most desirable woman in the world. And rather than taking advantage she's been haranguing her, she's been bullying her, she's been making her miserable.

With this revelation comes the sickening feeling that rather than undoing the buttons of Rochelle's mind she's been sawing away at her psyche with an angle grinder.

'Oh but let's not talk about that' cries Sandra. 'Let's talk about you!'

This is the final insult to a terrible evening. With a cry Rochelle rises to her feet and threads her way through the crowded restaurant. For an instant Sandra is paralysed. Then she too leaps up and makes her way out. Following a tense scene where the waiter, who followed her out, accuses her of welching on her bill, Sandra has flung many notes in the man's annoying face and now searches desperately for Rochelle.

She knows Rochelle takes the train home. She knows Rochelle has some sort of weird connection with Stanley Spencer. Spencer lived West, so her train presumably departs from Marylebone. Yet had Sandra dashed off in the direction of Marylebone she would have been disappointed. In fact Rochelle hasn't gone far. She has taken refuge on a wooden bench with an inscription reading 'To mark Paula and Debbie's civil partnership, 2008. From their many friends.'

Sandra, her mind working overtime, her head flicking toe and froe, has her attention caught by a couple of people stopping apparently to help someone in distress. She hurriedly joins them and sees Rochelle, hunched on her bench, sobbing brokenly.

'Need a doctor?' asks the women. Sandra pushes them out the way.

'The only thing this woman needs' she proclaims. 'Is me.'

Sandra can be grateful for whatever intuition caused her to utter those words. She couldn't know that those words are *exactly the same* as the sentence that has run a hundred times through Rochelle's confused and hopeful mind. Hearing them, all the pain and confusion of the restaurant is wiped clean like a waiter's cloth on a soiled cocktail table. She springs up and the two women meet in an embrace usually reserved for the honeymoon.

'Oh darling!' moans Sandra, caring nothing that her work persona is definitely blown.

'I love you I love you!' cries Rochelle, having also watched the same doomed 1940s romance on the TV, and preferring the simple sentiment to the more emotionally complex speeches.

'Fantastic!' respond the women, applauding, before moving on with their own evening.

'I don't care about dumb Alec' says Sandra. 'I only want to make you happy.'

'I'll find out everything there is to know' Rochelle continues. ' I'll be your spy. I'll help you bring down Alec. I'll do it out of love!'

Sandra considers for a beat.

'Okay. Thanks.'

Then emotion overwhelms them both and they sink down onto the bench that marks Paula and Debbie making it official. Neither can think of any place they would prefer to be.

Nineteen. ALEC & OTHERS

Alec has been dreading this day. Adam is scheduled to leave hospital and travel 90 miles to the care home where he will be incarcerated. Darryl, to Alec's surprise, has visited Adam virtually every day, bringing little gifts from the outside world he's shoplifted. He keeps up Adam's spirits with stories of wild Soho, snippets of who's doing who, why and how much they benefited monetarily. Yet Darryl is a creature of Soho and once Adam is out of sight, Alec knows he will be forgotten.

Alec has spent time on the phone ensuring that the care home knows Alec is willing to foot any extra bills for Adam. He's paid extra for a single room, for a private bathroom and a TV. Yet he's conscious that Adam is a frail, vulnerable young man, and he wishes he could do more. However, the simple circumstances of being Chair of Bland & Co. prevent him from considering a move out of London, so he tells himself he must be content with what he can accomplish financially.

He drops by Dennis's office and is told by Philip that Dennis has not been seen the last hour. He asks Sandra's PA where *she* is and the PA gives him a blank stare. Meanwhile, in a café that has discreet booths, Dennis and Sandra are embroiled in conspiracy.

'It's not enough. Yes we've got sexism and possibly racism but it's still not enough. You must remember, Dennis, that most of the board of Bland thinks the words sexism and racism are highly amusing. They certainly don't take them seriously.'

'So what are our options? I'm getting to the stage where I automatically think of myself as Chair and then I see that monstrous figure lumbering down the corridor and I remember I'm not. It's not good for my mental health. I'm worried my obsession with Alec will cause me to be careless with figures.'

'Yes. I couldn't help overhearing that you've got a meeting with an insurance rep. Increasing your personal work indemnity?'

Dennis stares hard at Sandra. 'Can I trust you with a little secret?'

'Of course' says Sandra, and being a good Catholic girl she crosses her fingers under the table while whispering 'not'.

'I recently was witness to a terrible death. It's really rattled me. I no longer feel confident. Therefore I'm going to treble my life insurance.'

'And make me your beneficiary?' asks Sandra eagerly. Dennis glares.

'I'm not leaving my money to you or anyone' he answers rudely. 'Don't you see? It's symbolic. It shows I take extra care of myself.'

'But,' says Sandra, never willing to let such matters go without a tussle, 'don't you think you should know who you're leaving your money to? Otherwise it will only go to the government and look what they'll do with it!'

Dennis regards Sandra balefully. 'Frankly you're the last person I'd name. Wouldn't be able to sleep for images of you breaking in and smothering me with my own pillow.'

Sandra considers. 'You know, once there might have been something in that. Not now. I've been a bit of a bitch, I know, but only because I felt so unloved and empty. Now I have someone. I'm sitting here with you in this place but in my heart I'm dancing naked in the mountains with my beloved.'

'You do sound different' agrees Dennis. 'You sound insane.'

'Oh! Just because your own heart is calcified doesn't mean that applies to everyone.'

'Actually, I did have someone I was keen on. It went horribly wrong. How does that song go? 'I'll never fall in love again?'

A short time later finds Dennis being informed he has a visitor. The visitor enters, his hand held out in welcome. Dennis was expecting the usual sort of flaccid middle-aged man and is taken aback by the vision of fresh youth that agrees to take a seat opposite him.

'I'm Ted' says the visitor. 'I'm here to fix you up good and proper.'

For the next 25 minutes Dennis's ears are assaulted with figures, facts, clauses and circumstances in which no pay out will be made. Dennis gets through the ordeal by staring at Ted's perfectly formed lips, his finely chiselled brow, and as much as he can see of his slim yet buff torso. He then gloomily moves on to assessing the likelihood that this tasty morsel is in any way available. He carries an atmosphere of being wrapped in cellophane, of never having entered a Soho bar or paid for a sleazy hour.

What is happening to Dennis is that, from having plummeted into the depths of Jerry's sordid world and attempted to clean it with a scrubbing brush, he has, although up till this moment not been aware of it, been craving innocence. Dennis sees that Ted has stopped talking and is now regarding him with a disappointed look, which grows greater with every second that Dennis says nothing.

'I'm so sorry' says Dennis, attempting to save the moment, 'I was miles away.'

'Yeah' responds Ted miserably, 'that's what they all say. Oh well.'

He begins to pack his brochures with the air of a man who's done this many times before and expects to do it many times more.

'Wait!' cries Dennis. 'I'm so sorry. I'll take ….' Here he gestures to take in the whole of Ted's presentation, 'I'll take everything. Thank you. I really do want to feel more secure.'

Ted's face lights up as only a man on commission-only will. 'Oh sick' he says. 'I can't tell you what this will do for me. I mean for you.'

It's the vulnerability Ted is showing, the spontaneous and indiscreet acknowledgment of his shaky status that causes Dennis to throw work caution to the wind. Yes, Ted is not exhibiting any signs of being gay, yes he might have a lovely blonde girlfriend, but Dennis can't bring the meeting to a close without at least indicating his interest.

'Why don't we settle arrangements and I'll sign over dinner?'

Ted freezes. Part of the comprehensive and thorough 15-minute briefing all reps from his company must undergo focused on inappropriate blurring of boundaries. It is frowned on for those offering a professional insurance service to include their body to seal the deal. The manager's exact words were 'And make sure you keep your pants on. We're not covered for sex pest complaints.'

As we are already aware, Ted has had one important relationship in his young life. That was winding down before Guy took a tumble and ended it abruptly. He then tried out a relationship with a much older man for size and was thoroughly disappointed and put off. The man in front of him now is somewhere in his late 30's. He's particularly impressed with Dennis's beautiful fingernails.

'I'll have dinner with you. But I warn you. I don't do one-night stands.'

Dennis glances guiltily at the open door behind Ted. Fortunately there is no one lingering in the corridor, one of the best sources of Dennis's own office intel.

'Romantic dinner,' mutters Dennis, just loud enough to reach Ted's ears, 'and I'll sign my insurance papers.'

After Ted has left the office, which to Dennis feels like the soul and meaning of his life walking away, he finds himself whistling a little tune. With a gentle smile he realises it's *I'll Never Fall in Love Again.*

In the last verse the singer says they won't ever fall in love again – until tomorrow. Tomorrow, he hopes, is today.

Which is all very sweet but doesn't help Alec, assailed by severe stomach cramps, who has joined Darryl at Adam's bedside.

'Promise me you'll call me at least once a week' he begs.

'Alec, sweetie, I'll have bugger all to do. I'll call you all the time. Believe me you'll get so sick of me.'

'You can also call me' says Darryl. 'As long as whoever owns this phone I found doesn't cancel the sim card.'

'We won't forget you' cries Alec, with tears in his eyes, as the efficient care home staff wheel Alec's bed out of the ward, down the lift and onto the ramp. Here an ambulance waits, doors open like a steel shark, waiting to engulf Adam's frail form.

'Don't forget' cries Darryl. 'If you meet any cute male nurses you can still give them oral!'

This is not the sort of low suggestion Alec believes is appropriate. Almost doubled over with stomach pain he still wishes to end this sad parting on a high note.

'I'll try to get down to you as regularly as possible. At least every fortnight.'

Adam is having a painful time being moved. He smiles wanly and waves listlessly.

'At least you've still got use of your hands' says Darryl brightly. 'If you get extra lucky you can do oral *and* handies at the same time.'

‘Oh for heaven’s sake, Darryl’ snaps Alec. ‘Can’t you ever stop thinking about sex?’

Darryl regards Alec balefully. ‘I do. Whenever I look at you.’

‘Please don’t fight’ says Adam. ‘You’re my two best friends in the world.’

‘Only friends’ adds Darryl. The porters begin to wheel Adam’s gurney into the ambulance.

‘Oh!’ cries Darryl. ‘If only I wasn’t about to be evicted again. If only I had a nice little one bedroom where I could look after Adam at home.’

Alec is occupied discreetly brushing tears from his eyes. Now he perks up.

‘Do you mean that? I’ve been impressed that you’ve visited him so often, but would you look after him on a daily basis?’

‘Don’t these hands look like the hands of a natural carer?’ snaps Darryl, snapping off one of his acrylic nails for emphasis.

Alec literally smites his own brow. ‘Ow!’ he says. ‘Of course. I’m making myself miserable because I didn’t want to take responsibility for Adam. But that doesn’t mean someone else couldn’t look after him in my home!’

Darryl rolls his eyes. ‘Duuh, grandpa!’

Alec thinks. The responsibility will be huge. Ongoing. And yet. Surely a broken leg heals at some point?

‘Hold the gurney’ he cries. The attendants look confused.

‘That ambulance is not going out of London. It’s going to my home. Number 3, Cheyney Crescent, Hampstead.’

‘But do you have sufficient room?’ asks Darryl.

‘I have eleven bedrooms’ replies Alec simply.

‘Damn you woman’ responds Darryl, who is only ever one quick scheme ahead of sleeping on cardboard under a bridge. ‘In that case I’ll never leave. Eleven bedrooms!’

Alec has grown to be fond of Darryl, yet he hesitates. Something about Darryl implies that although it’s easy to get him to move into one’s home, ejecting him might take an armed intervention. He proceeds cautiously.

‘Uh, one of the bedrooms is more of a box room.’

‘I’ll take it!’

The porters agree to drive the ambulance to Alec’s home. Alec agrees to Darryl moving in. And just like that, Alec’s stomach condition miraculously disappears.

Twenty. ALEC & CO

Alec, having organised a makeshift invalid's quarters, having cancelled the expensive room outside London and had a bitter argument about their refunding his various deposits, returns to Bland's. At home Darryl has moved into not so much the box room as the best guest suite on the first floor. The one that has its own bathroom and adjoining boudoir. His eyes lit up with barely suppressed excitement, Darryl tours Alec's palatial residence, his practised eyes spotting various *objets* and easily portable goods. In his mind's eye he's already visiting various dubious antique dealers of his acquaintance and explaining how he was left the goods by a distant relative who died and doesn't want them back.

Dennis and Ted meet for dinner, then Ted accompanies him back to Dennis's home. The next morning Dennis climbs naked out of his bed. Ted lies on his back, watching him through eyes half-closed with satisfaction and happiness. For the last couple of minutes, while Dennis plays idly with his hair, Ted has been calculating how much of the wardrobe space Dennis will be willing to give up once he's moved in.

'I can get my jazz over this evening' he says, startling Dennis. Standing with one foot balanced while he slides into his boxers Dennis isn't sure he's heard correctly. 'What jazz, darling?' he asks, sliding the boxers into place and automatically adjusting his genitals.

'All my jazz' replies Ted. Dennis opens a drawer and extracts a clean shirt.

'What jazz?' he says again, his mind still not woken from its bath of sexual fulfilment.

'When I met Guy I moved in the first day. Well, the day after the first night.'

'Moved in?' asks Dennis in genuine horror.

'Yeah' responds Ted. 'I told you I wasn't someone who does one-night stands. It has to be serious. Were you lying to me?'

Dennis shakes his head. 'Ted, I like you a lot. But. I mean, if you hadn't met me, where would you be living?'

'Oh. My late ex didn't leave a will so it's going to take ages for me to get my half of our place. They're changing the locks today.'

'You mean you planned this? You're trying to use me?' asks Dennis, rightly shocked to the core after many years of him being the user.

'No way. I was going to move in with my gran. But she hates me and she's a total fascist so I just thought since you said all that to me last night you'd want me to move in. You did, if you remember, say you never wanted to sleep without me again.'

'Uh. That was one of those. Uh, things men say, when they're having a good time. It's what's said in the cold morning light you have to listen to.'

Ted's happy expression snaps off and a hurt light illuminates his eyes. 'Oh right. So you're just another one of *those*.'

Ted throws off the covers and slides lithely to a standing position. He pulls on his trousers, shoves his underpants into a back pocket.

'Look, honey' says Dennis, glancing at his watch. 'We can talk more about this later.'

Ted concentrates on retrieving his other possessions before speaking.

'Meet me for a drink tonight' says Dennis.

'I don't need you to buy me drinks. I thought we were on the same page.'

'We are, darling. But no one meets someone one day and moves in the next. It's asking for trouble.'

'I'm not asking for anything' snaps Ted.

'Yes, you are! You're asking me to let you into my daily life.'

'I thought last night you said that was what you wanted!'

Dennis pauses, guiltily. He is not so hungover from alcohol and hours of exhausting sex that he can't remember what he said. It is simply that having moved in scurrilous circles for so many years he's amazed to meet a gay man who actually believes what he tells them.

'Ted, come on. Let's have breakfast.'

Ted stomps off to the bathroom and Dennis sends a text to Philip saying he's been delayed. Dennis reckons that once Ted's had a proper breakfast he'll think more logically.

'Let's splurge on breakfast' is his greeting as Ted hurtles back from the bathroom, his hair now dampened down and properly parted.

'Just forget it' cries Ted as he half drags on his jacket and makes for the front door. To Dennis's amazement the young man seems serious about leaving. So surprised is Dennis that by the time he opens the door recently slammed by Ted, Ted is part way down the road. Dennis is aware that he has not put on socks and shoes. And that the pavements outside his home tend to be sticky with an unknown substance that leaks from the drains. Instead of following on foot he shouts 'Was it something I said?'

This is a line someone once told him she said to a man who having spent the night with her abruptly left when she asked him if he'd thought about the names of future children. Dennis thought it was funny. He hopes Ted will see the funny side. Ted doesn't even turn round. If anything he speeds up his departure, crossing the road and turning the corner.

'You little bastard' says Dennis to himself. 'Glad I'm out of that one' he tells himself. Although, as he returns to his home and throws the bed into some sort of apple pie order, he has the grace to acknowledge 'Damn. Didn't appreciate what I had. And now it's gone.' Like the Dodo, which was a gentle bird wanting only to be left alone to graze grass, his thinking continues, my hopes of a decent relationship with a sweet man are dead. He sighs. Then he becomes aware that he probably needs to find another purveyor of insurance and he sighs again.

Later the same day, after work, in a different location, Sandra sits on her sofa, Rochelle lying in her lap. She plays idly with Rochelle's hair. They are in that stage of a relationship where people give each other affectionate, intimate names.

'PeePee?' says Sandra. PeePee is short for Pretty Princess, which is Rochelle's new soubriquet.

'Yes, oh Queen?' Sandra's nickname is Queen of the Universe.

'I feel like I'm my own age, plus in gay age I'm three days old. I feel split between two separate and unconnected timelines.'

Rochelle regards her beloved with eyes misty with affection. 'I know. I suppose this is what they call coming out.'

'Coming out. It's never too late.'

'We're so lucky, in a way' says Rochelle, which is touching since life has been unusually cruel towards her until now. 'We're old enough to know what we want, and now we've got everything we need.'

‘PeePee’ says Sandra, ‘are we going to come out at work?’

There’s a silence. ‘Queen’, says Rochelle, ‘Don’t you think it makes our love even more special if we keep it a secret?’

‘I know’ replies Sandra, ‘But I’ve never had someone I want to show off before. I don’t like the idea of men looking at you and thinking you’re available. And, on a different matter, I think you can stop wearing booby dresses now. You’ve caught me.’

Rochelle raises herself up on one arm. ‘You’re not going to be one of those jealous women who wants to stop me living my life my way, are you?’

‘Would you like me to be?’

‘Definitely not.’

‘So, we’re not going to come out at work and you’re going to keep offering up your magnificent breasts to every office worker, delivery boy and the man who waters the plants?’

‘Yes.’

‘Oh PeePee, you’re tougher than you look’ sighs Sandra, frustrated though impressed.

‘You make me tougher’ responds Rochelle. ‘When I see me through your eyes, I like what I see.’

‘Is this how our evenings are going to be?’ asks Sandra.

‘What do you mean, Queen?’

‘I mean are we going to sit around for five hours and talk about feelings?’

In reply Rochelle rises, grasps Sandra’s hand and pulls her towards the ever-welcome bedroom door.

'No wait' says Sandra. 'You can't use sex every time the conversation gets intense.'

Rochelle considers this thoughtfully. 'Why not?'

For the rest of the night Sandra racks her brain to come up with a convincing argument. She eventually decides that she'll wait a few years and see if a counter-argument ever naturally presents itself.

Twenty-One. ADAM & CO

A rehabilitation nurse from the hospital drops in to explain the mysteries of bed baths to Alec and Darryl. Alec wants to write it all down but he can't find his silver pen or his crocodile skin notepad. Fortunately the nurse brings pages of helpful diagrams together with simple instructions. She also leaves a supply of soaps and foam and sponge applicators. After she goes Alec is concerned because they seem to have disappeared but after an exhaustive search they turn up in Darryl's room.

A few days later Darryl is startled to see Alec making notes in a notepad. The last time he saw that silver pen and crocodile skin pad he was handing them over to one of his contacts in exchange for several small snap bags partially full of white powder. Hearing his gasp, Alec lowers his pen and explains.

'Darryl, the moment items began to go missing I hired a combination personal shopper/private detective. He's pricey but not as pricey as a live-in professional carer. You are managing Adam's care adequately and you at least have genuine feeling for him. What we can do, if you care to agree, is that if you continue to look after Adam I will, on a weekly basis, put fifteen hundred pounds – minus room and board – in your bank account. And you won't need to steal any more. Do we have a deal?'

With a shock Darryl realises that since he's moved in to take care of Adam, he's not only completely forgotten that he actually still has a job, he's also not spent any money online. That is how entirely he has taken to devoting himself to Adam's welfare. He checks his bank account. He'd never realised that the numbers can appear without a minus sign on the right.

And, as Alec notes, one of the plus points to Darryl's many, many moves is that he is unusually adept at being comfortable in someone else's home. Because of Alec's devotion to running Bland's he has never taken an interest in the enormous home he inherited from his father. Alison's only personality quirk was her obsession with being the house's cleaner. Since her death Alec has let the house begin to fall apart around him. Since Darryl's arrival this has begun to be reversed, since when Adam is sleeping Darryl needs something to do. He began with the library, converted into Adam's bedroom, and has then cleaned his own and Alec's bedroom. The rest of the house remains in the grip of dust, cobwebs and mysterious damp patches and it is this neglect, when Philip arrives to visit Adam, that has the most effect on him. It appears to Philip that Alec is down on his luck. Philip has never known if Bland's was actually profitable, or whether old man Bland, Alec's father, kept the place going as a vanity project. Therefore he doesn't like to put Alec to any financial expense and refuses everything in the way of refreshments he is offered, accepting only a glass of cold water.

Philip looks on disapproving as Darryl, in his guise of carer/chatelaine, opens a fine bottle of red and splashes generous glassfuls for himself and Alec.

'You're Adam's best friend and you work for Bland's' concludes Darryl, after having stared at him for some time. 'I feel like I know you but you're also a blank.'

'Everyone says I'm a blank' notes Philip. 'I think my own mother couldn't pick me out of a police line-up.'

There's no one reason why this should be true. Philip is slight and stands with his shoulders lightly bent over. His dark hair is kept neat and clear of his ears, which are a normal size and shape. His mouth is neither thin nor sensuous, his nose neither long, pointed or scarred by a break. His eyes, if anyone cares to look, are actually a delightful brown with flicks of gold, like Tiger's Eye. Yet no one has bothered to look for some time and the ones who do usually don't last. Philip's life is an unhappy balance of not being good at his job at work, and not being comfortable in his private life. The one true friend he has held onto through life's travails is Adam.

'Come on,' says Darryl cheerfully, 'Philip you can help give our patient a bed bath.'

'I really wouldn't like to' says Philip, thinking of how seeing his friend's body, vulnerable and naked, would cause all manner of emotional and sexual confusions to bounce around inside him.

'Don't be a sissy' says Darryl. 'I do wonders with this towel. He's naked, yes, and you're embarrassed yes, but you'll see less of Adam's privates in his bed bath than you would if he forgot to do up his zip after a quiet slash. I model my technique on old burlesque fan dancers.'

While applying a warm, wet, soapy sponge to Adam, Darryl also likes to talk.

'You're quite repressed, sexually, aren't you?' he enquires, while carefully sponging the back of Adam's neck.

'I would say I am' say Alec and Philip in spontaneous unison.

Darryl, holding the sponge, pauses. 'Which of you wants to go first? I know nothing about either of you so it'll all be a glorious surprise.'

'I'll start' says Philip. 'I wouldn't say I was sexually repressed, more that I like a particular sort of man. But for some reason they don't like me.'

'Yeah' butts in Darryl, 'I know what you mean. I like rich, hung, uncut, handsome studs who believe in spoiling a girl. '

'I'm pretty easy going and I'm willing to compromise' says Philip.

‘Me too. They don’t have to be uncut’ agrees Darryl, moving the soapy sponge to do Adam’s armpits. ‘One of the saddest facts of life is the rich hung studs are phenomenally stingy and ungenerous.’

‘No’ says Philip, ‘that’s not *my* type.’

As with most comments made by Philip, this one appears to hover in the air for a moment, then evaporate. One hears of people whose every passing thought, whose lightest and most vapid witticism is immediately written down and shared universally. One is thinking here of the late Prince Philip. Our Philip, alas, sits on the other end of the spectrum where no one seems able to find the will or energy to even acknowledge that he’s said something, let alone scribe it into immortality.

Philip gives up his efforts to contribute to the gathering. It’s a fact that after people have been with him, if they are the introspective sort who review the encounter just gone, they may recall that Philip did say things, yet they cannot remember what they were. He has taken to social media in an attempt to make his mark as an individual. Yet he can’t get above 20 Twitter followers and half of those are governmental bots. Even LinkedIn have stopped sending him unsuitable suggestions for potential new employment.

Alec waits until it’s clear Philip has stopped speaking. ‘In my case I’m not so much repressed as it has been forbidden my whole life. First my disgusting father, then he handed over the reins to my late wife. Who is entirely blameless: she simply didn’t know what she was getting.’

Conversation stops while Darryl manipulates the towel so he can clean Adam’s chest and stomach without any unwanted sexual implications. When he moves onto Adam’s legs Alec continues.

‘I remember there was one time. I must have been 16. Our local tobacconist’s had a top shelf I would discreetly examine with my eyes scrolled upwards while I appeared to be examining the shelf beneath.

The one, it turned out, that featured women's magazines. No wonder they use to look at me funny. Anyway, one day I moved a couple of magazines around while the shopkeeper's back was turned, and to my amazement discovered there was a second layer of magazines. These, and just thinking about it now my cheeks blush and my heart quickens, were American musclemen periodicals. I remember there was one particular title: *DemiGods*. You might imagine handsome Vikings with enormous muscles but no, these were charming young men with sweet, welcoming smiles, posed in bathing suits or with their legs hiding anything too shocking.'

Darryl picks up a different towel and begins to dry Adam. 'Yeah, that's often the way guys begin. Starts with muscles or sweet smiles, then you move on to what you're really attracted to. In my case it's men who can pay for dinner.'

'Oh, just thinking back of the man on that cover. I instantly decided I must have this magazine or die. But how to get it past the gimlet eye of the shopkeeper?'

'You can just buy them, you know' says Adam, lying on his back, enjoying the warm wet sponge making him clean and fresh.

'I couldn't buy it! The shopkeeper was a stooge of my father's!'

'So what did you do?' asks Darryl, intrigued, the hand with the sponge poised and dripping on Adam.

'Only one thing for it. I bought another magazine. That was put in a brown paper bag. I then returned to the magazine display, lay the brown paper bag down, lifted *DemiGods* off the shelf and when the shopkeeper wasn't looking I whisked it into the brown paper bag.'

Darryl looks at Alec with his mouth slightly open. 'That's brilliant! I've never thought of that!'

‘On my way out I placed a five pound note on the counter. I told the shopkeeper I’d found it on the floor and it wasn’t mine. He was a revolting person, I’ve no doubt he immediately pocketed it.’

‘So then you were free to enjoy the magazine?’ asks Darryl.

‘Well, of course I had to tell myself I wasn’t reading it because I was … I had to tell myself a story. I was interested in men only because I didn’t have a girlfriend. And I needed to look through the pages carefully, one by one, in order to decide which of the men featured I wanted to be.’

‘And then you wanked?’ asks Darryl, never afraid to jump to the punchline.

‘Absolutely not! These were gods, after all. My viewing of them was entirely reverent.’

‘And that was the only time you thought you might be gay?’

‘Oh no, I knew entirely. But any idea of that sort of life passed by on the other side of the street. I’ve been one of life’s natural celibates.’

‘So that’s what you are now, basically?’ says Adam.

‘No. Now I’m someone who will never get back those stolen years’ says Alec, solemnly. ‘Perhaps if I could have been myself just once I would be content. Yet feeling my true self was denied all those years, I now feel as though I will never be able to make up for what I’ve lost. Just throwing good after bad.’

This confession coincides with Darryl needing to turn Adam on his side so some of its profundity is lost. Yet it remains in the air like a sweet, dead smell.

‘I know you think I’m someone with my shit together’ says Darryl, once he has finished the complicated part of the sponge bath. Philip and Alec, who have never thought of Darryl like this look at him, somewhat startled, yet Darryl is beginning to be lost in his own reverie and has stopped reading his audience.

'But there was a time I was as pure as … whatever's pure nowadays, I can't keep up with these internet so-called influencers, they all look 13 to me.' Darryl sighs.

'And there was a time I was 13. I was a prodigy. People said I was the most exquisite boy dancer they had ever seen. It was predicted I would do great things in the world of ballet. My turn-out was particularly admired. I got a scholarship to Vanne's Ballet School. Mr Vanne was a retired former principal dancer with one of the top ballet companies. And, from the age of 14, he was my lover.'

'Good heavens' says Alec.

'He told me that we would be like Diaghilev and Nijinsky. That he would return to the world of commercial ballet and mount shows featuring me. He even described creating a truly revolutionary *Swan Lake*, with me as a male Odette/Odile.' Here Darryl's eyes mist over. 'Can you imagine' he says in a deeper tone, 'how wonderful it would have been if the world could see *Swan Lake* danced by two men?'

Alec is fairly sure he has read about something along these lines, he rather thinks it was choreographed by Sir Matthew Bourne, but he doesn't wish to interrupt Darryl's flow of painful memories.

'For two years I danced and loved with Mr Vanne. Then my parents moved us away. For three years I wrote to him, I dreamed of the life we would have together once I could make my way back to him. Finally, when I was 19, I was able to get myself back down to London. I didn't tell him I was arriving, I just knew, because I'd imagined it so many times, that when he saw me he would drop whatever he was doing and embrace me. And tell me he would never let me go.'

Darryl, with sad and heavy hand, finishes Adam's bath, deftly removing the towel and flicking the blanket back onto him in one smooth movement. He takes his time to continue and the others realise he is also preparing them for the big reveal.

'He was working in his office. I threw open the door, my heart full, my face radiant with joy and desire. He looked at me. Then he went back to his work. I couldn't believe what had just happened. I stood in the door, feeling foolish and desperate. He looked up at me and said, these words, so cruel and final, I want to die now like I wanted to die then:

'You've got too old, Darryl. I don't need you anymore.'

'You see' says Darryl, carefully lifting the bowl of water, 'he was a paedophile. He'd never loved me. He loved only my 14-year-old body.' Darryl removes the bowl of water. From the kitchen the others hear the splash of water hitting the sink and draining away. Philip looks at Alec and Adam.

'I really didn't think Darryl was like that' says Philip.

'It shows you none of us know the history of another person' says Alec, pleased to have a reason to wax philosophically. In his own youth he'd been good at rationalising thwarted desires, now here was an opportunity to show the two young ones how one manages to live with despair and disappointment.

'You know, we all see the person in front of us and imagine that's how they've always been. For example, I know when the two of you look at me, you see this 'loveable old walrus'. But just as Darryl was once a vulnerable, betrayed youth, so was I once as lithe and smooth as you are now.'

Darryl returns with another, already opened, bottle of red and everyone but Philip has a top up. Even Adam, who lays on his back with his eyes silently filled with tears.

'You're crying' says Darryl. 'Was it something I said?'

'I've made such a mess of stuff' answers Adam. 'I never set out to be a rent boy. I mean, I know I fancy it up by offering massages, but I do them on my bed. I can't be bothered to save up the money for a proper massage table. Or to get properly qualified. I'm a mess.'

'Is that what you'd like to do?' asks Alec. 'I have no objection in putting you through a professional physiotherapy qualification. As your adopted grandfather, I think I'd enjoy it.'

Adam smiles, his tiredness showing through his young complexion. 'Thanks but I'm crap at it. I'm barely surviving on my looks. It's just that I've never wanted to *be* anything. That's what happens when you don't know what you want to be. You become what's left once all the proper jobs have been filled.'

'I suppose, since I do have a proper job and we're getting ready for the annual meeting of the board, I should go home' says Philip. It takes a while for what he's said to filter through to the others, so Philip has already retrieved his coat and is making for the front door before the others react. He won't be stopped so they kiss him goodnight and he disappears into the darkness.

Alec and Darryl finish the new bottle. Alec watches as Darryl switches off the lights in the rooms they aren't using.

'What?' asks Darryl.

'Nothing. It's interesting to see the way you take care of this old place. I usually wake up in the morning and the rooms are a blaze of light. I'm sure it's highly wasteful but I can't be bothered to save electricity when I can't save myself.'

'Oh, you're not doing so badly' says Darryl lightly. 'I mean – 10 bedrooms!'

'Don't forget, I inherited this pile. I inherited Bland & Co. I've always been a dutiful son and I hate myself and my life' responds Alec.

Darryl tries to think of something positive to say but the only thing that comes is a half-quote about the peace and silence of the grave, which seems too near the knuckle, so he busies himself tidying. Then the two say goodnight to Adam and begin to ascend the grand wooden staircase up to their separate bedrooms.

'It was fun this evening' calls Darryl over his shoulder. 'I think I understand you a bit better now.'

'Yes' replies Alec, 'And I you.'

'Oh, forget that stuff I told you' says Darryl. 'I think I was just being sentimental. I never get a chance to just hang out with some sympathetic guys.'

'Me neither. I kept having the wish that this evening would go on forever, that I would never have to return alone to my room. That we could all just talk about ourselves, and that there would always be some kind ear to listen.'

At the door of his room Darryl turns and looks at Alec. He's never been fonder of the older fellow. 'You're a very brave man' he calls. 'I hope it all works out for you.'

'Thank you' says Alec, and swiftly opens his door, moves through it, and closes it gently.

Darryl watches him go, and smiles. How amazing: the three of them under the same roof. For how long Darryl doesn't know. Long and hard experience tells him that although the bad times manage to cling on, the good times are apt to disappear in a trice. He's never known what a trice is and thinks it must be like a tricycle, which you peddle away at top speed. However, it felt good to talk tonight. Hopefully, before the inevitable harsh ending, there will again be times like this.

Twenty-Two. ENSEMBLE

The day of Bland & Co's annual board meeting dawns bright and sharp. An interesting coincidence thinks Dennis, who intends to be both bright and sharp in the meeting. Yesterday representatives from around the globe jetted into London at their own expense and are now finishing breakfast at their individual luxury hotels. Dennis stands at the door of Sandra's office. Sandra has made a list of the ammunition they have to take down Alec. Alas, however many times she rearranges the words 'sexism' and 'racism' she can't get really excited. She is a little startled by how excited Dennis appears to be.

'A miracle' proclaims Dennis. 'Ask and ye shall find' he follows, which is more than Sandra does.

'Sorry, what are you burbling on about?'

'This morning, not ten minutes ago, I received information that will smash through Alec's defences and leave him helpless, like a giant turtle flipped over on its back.'

'So tell.'

'No. It's too good. I know exactly how I'm going to play my attack.'

'You always prefer me to go through strategy with you.'

'Not this time. I want to see the look in your eyes when I destroy a fifty-year career in a few sentences. I expect it to be a look of blind and permanent surrender to my brilliance.'

Now Sandra is also excited, yet she cannot get Dennis to share his hot new revelations. She treats herself to a few quick words and a hurried squeeze with her beloved, then proceeds to the boardroom to greet the overseas arrivals. She admires the good job HR have done in making the boardroom both celebratory and austere. As always, the dignity of the company is sacrosanct and of paramount importance. To take down the old buzzard here! If Alec can be regarded as a werewolf, Sandra hopes the bullets in Dennis's metaphorical gun are solid 925 silver.

Sandra joins others who are admiring the centrepiece of HR's festive decorations, a colourful selection of just some of the items Bland's is responsible for unleashing on a gullible world. If you have ever visited a holy shrine and, wandering into the gift shop, found your attention drawn by a six-foot plastic inflatable St John the Baptist, chances are you are already aware of the goods purveyed by Bland's, one of the world's leading manufacturers, distributors and promoters of Christian ephemera. From little bottles of holy water, through pictures of Our Lady with a clock in her immaculate stomach, to puzzles that, when assembled, make a charming picture of The Last Supper or The Crucifixion, there isn't an incident or figure in The Bible not exploited by Bland's. Sandra lifts one of the season's hottest sellers, a 3-dimensional depiction of Christ which, when you move it, turns into an image of former president Trump in a similarly martyred pose. A label modestly notes that they've sold thousands in the rural areas of the US.

'How lovely' murmurs a soft voice to her left and Sandra smiles at the wrinkled, saintly figure of Mother Agnes.

'Mother Agnes' says Sandra, dipping one leg as though being presented to Royalty which, when you think about it, Mother is. 'How wonderful as always to see you.' Mother Agnes reaches out a wizened hand to bestow a blessing on Sandra. Then the same hand picks up a snow globe featuring Jesus in the Temple and gives it a good shake, admiring the fake, swirling snow that has somehow got into the temple.

'Please take the snow globe as our gift to you, Mother' says Sandra reverently. Mother Agnes doesn't reply, she merely tucks the snow globe into her capacious handbag, already bulging with free loot to take back and distribute among the deserving poor of her parish. Mother

Agnes may believe she's manifesting the spirit of the Holy Ghost but in reality it's Darryl she's channelling.

Dennis arrives a couple of minutes later. Sandra eyes him carefully as he scopes out the room. It's vital that there are sufficient board members to make up a quorum. If his new intel *is* dynamite it will be most destructive if sufficient of the board is present to vote Alec into hell and damnation.

The unwitting potential recipient of the worst Dennis can unleash has enjoyed a simple breakfast of buttered toast and tea and now prepares to undergo, as he has always seen it, the very worst day of his work year. From the time that his sadistic father brought him into the family business Alec has barely tolerated the nature of the work. Endless meetings with dignitaries from around the world who look to Bland's to do their proselyting for them. A nicely conceived piece of kitsch, so Bland's has always believed although never using that word, can convert hundreds of thousands and is worth a great deal to the offerings box. It is one of life's ironies that Bland senior, a man of no positive emotions and many negatives ones, has gained a worldwide reputation for saintliness by suppling religious iconography to the world's most sacred Christian sites. Perhaps it had something to do with the ruthless undercutting and sabotage of other suppliers, yet that would be only one dirty trick employed by Bland senior.

There is an expectant buzz of conversation from the worthy religious representatives gathered, as well as the unworthy business-suited, sketchy types who have found Bland's merchandise helpful in solving their ongoing money laundering conundrum. Arriving just on time, having given himself a stern talking to in front of the mirror in the men's room, Alec takes his usual place at the head of the table. This familiar ritual is greeted by Dennis with an enhanced twist to his already pursed mouth.

The minutes are presented and passed. Alec efficiently runs through the agenda. Whilst the various minor matters are being dealt with Alec is aware that Sandra and Dennis keep exchanging significant glances. He wonders which of the agenda items is the cause. He is relieved when the end of the agenda is in sight. Only AOB remains.

'Any Other Business?' enquires Alec in a tone that hopes there is none.

A silence. Mother Agnes can be heard asking to be passed the biscuit plate. When no one is looking she adds the biscuits to her bulging handbag. No one is watching because everyone's attention is riveted on Dennis, who has introduced a spectacular, even unthinkable motion.

'I would like the board to vote on the following motion. That Alec Bland be immediately replaced as Chairman. Due to the sordid and licentious nature of his private life. A private life entirely at odds with the nobility and high nature of Bland & Co and everything we hold dear.'

Monseigneur de Val from the Lourdes outlet is the first to react.

'But what evidence do we have of this? We cannot take the word of this man. He may be a lunatic!'

'I'm no lunatic' replies Dennis soberly. 'I can prove everything I say. In fact, in this room is the very person who can verify my accusations!'

Philip had been wondering why, at the last minute, he had been asked to take the minutes rather than Rochelle, who is heartbroken at not being in her usual place besides Alec. With a flush he realises that Dennis, rather than being unusually and idly chatty this morning, has in fact been pumping Philip for details of Philip's visit to Alec. And Adam and Darryl. At the time Philip had been so relieved that his usually angry boss was evidently fascinated with the visit that he had gone into great, and now he realises, entirely indiscreet and inappropriate detail.

'Tell us, Philip, what you witnessed on your visit to Alec Bland's home last evening?'

Philip is thinking fast. He's thinking absolute denial is his best defence. He knows that a description of Alec's housemates will damn the dear man. It won't matter even if he fleshes out the characterisation by explaining Adam's charm, Darryl's innocent selfishness. Once named Alec will be shamed. And yet, denial isn't going to do the job. He can see Mother Agnes is regarding him like a mongoose eyeing an uncooperative baby snake. Up and down the table, Prelates, Archbishops, Vicars and members of various drug and gambling syndicates are expecting him to answer the question. It should also be remembered that many of Bland & Co's staff are attracted to the company because they cherish their own personal faith. Like Philip. Which makes them vulnerable to commands from so many of God's representatives on earth: they have no option but to speak.

'Uh. Mr Bland has a lovely home in a leafy part of North London.'

'This isn't a guided tour' snarls Dennis, 'tell us in precise detail exactly what Bland's housemates do for a living.'

There is a pause, during which Mother Agnes can be heard asking to be passed the other plate of biscuits.

'Well,' says Philip, 'there's Darryl. Darryl's kind of a T-Girl – that is a man who likes to dress and live as a woman. And there's Adam. His work name is Zac. Zac works as a sensual masseur for gay men.'

Philip is about to go on to explain that Adam isn't working at the moment because he broke his leg, and that Darryl has given up online poker and casual theft. But, like a witness in court who has been asked yes or no only, the mitigating factors are dismissed with a snort from Dennis.

‘A gay male masseur! A transvestite! Are these the sort of people we wish our Chair to consort with?’ This summation of the business at hand emerges not from Dennis but from Sandra. Up till now she has been stewing, brooding, wondering what big scandal Dennis has up his sleeve. Now that it’s out in the open, given that she intends to be made Managing Director, she believes its time the board heard from her.

‘I’m shocked. I’m more than shocked, I’m scandalised. I’m outraged. I’ve never heard such filth. I can only apologise to the board, many of whom have not until this moment even dreamed that such satanic creatures exist on God’s good earth. When I’m made Managing Director I will do my utmost to make this wonderful company great again. We may have fallen, as has our accursed Chair, but we will rise and we will be glorious.’

Sandra is aware, as she speaks, that she seems to be regurgitating snippets from various speeches from rabid right-wing politicians she has enjoyed listening to over the last couple of years. She is counting on getting across her general meaning, thus making the source material immaterial.

‘And when I am Chair’ crows Dennis, happy in knowing that since Ted he has been entirely celibate, ‘I swear we will purge the entire company of any and all whiff of scandal. Only the blameless, by which I mean the celibate or the married rather than living together in sin, will be tolerated as members of our sacred company. We have a God-anointed task to bring His artifacts and relics to His people, and as Chair I intend that task to be accomplished with a ruthlessness not seen since the days of The Inquisition.’

Hearing so many of their favourite buzz words the entire table can do no more than enthusiastically applaud. While applauding, they also shoot venomous looks in Alec’s direction. If he is relying on Christian charity and forgiveness he is going to need to look elsewhere.

A vote is swiftly taken. There are 22 people around the table, plus Alec and Philip who for different individual reasons are not invited to vote. There are 21 votes for immediate termination of Alec's position as Chair, and for Dennis and Sandra's new positions as Chair and Managing Director. The single holdout turns out to be the Archbishop of Lourdes who has fallen asleep and who, once the matter is explained, is revealed not to be a holdout in the slightest. It's a clean sweep of 22.

This is Dennis's moment. He is almost completely confident that his day is won. The tiny fly is that someone may, in some despicable way, know about his meaningless and, really, laughable and harmless dalliance with Ted. Yet he still feels basically impregnable, bolstered by the many years of hard sucking up to all the board members, who now regard him with a serene benevolence.

'So all that remains' says Dennis, 'is to boot this fallen creature out of the company.'

Alec pulls himself shakily to his feet. He begins to shamble out before stopping.

'There is something I would like to say to this board' he begins. 'You may see before you a man confident in his sexual orientation, yet I must emphasise that it has been at considerable personal cost. Does not the bible say 'know thyself?' How can it be wrong when that is what I have done?' The board, as one, shoot him looks which tell him in no uncertain terms that no one is in a mood to listen to philosophising. Shocked by such uniform anathema, Alec's words falter on his lips and wither. To everyone in the room he is a man rightfully shamed, about to be cast into the dustbin of the company's history.

To everyone except Philip. For the last few minutes, as he has been forced to tally the votes, Philip has been feeling just awful about inadvertently betraying not only his friends but also Alec, for whom he's always had a soft spot. Seeing the elderly man so bent, so humiliated, Philip breaks through a lifetime of speaking softly or not at all and rises with a purpose that, if not divine, is at least in defence of a good person.

'Actually, if I can understand what just happened, you've got rid of Alec because he doesn't fit into the company's high-minded moral code. Yes?'

'Absolutely' says Sandra, carefully shouting above everyone else in her new position as Managing Director.

'Then I'd like to say that Sandra is not fit for office either.'

A gasp runs round the already scandalised room.

'Not because she's a Lesbian' says Philip, looking Mother Agnes directly in the face, 'but because she's in breach of Item 43 of the company's employment contract. She is having an affair with another member of staff. Which is strictly prohibited.'

Part of Bland senior's religious mania drove him to construct employment contracts that went far further than what is currently legal. Yet because the company deals in religious artifacts Bland senior was able to include morals clauses usually confined to actual religious organisations.

As one the table swings its heads and merciless eyes in the direction of Sandra. Sandra wilts. She offers no argument. Instead, in another development that will be described in 22 written accounts of the morning as 'sensational', the door is thrown open and Rochelle, forced until now to listen from outside, rushes in and throws herself into Sandra's arms. Sandra automatically enfolds her beloved and kisses her ear tenderly. No further proof, in fact, is required.

'There is only one way forward now'. Dennis's voice cuts through the raised, and in some cases hysterical, voices filling the room. 'I move for the immediate termination of this woman's employment. I will act up as Managing Director as well as Chair.'

A little later Sandra has been persuaded to quit the room. She doesn't go very far, merely taking a place, with Rochelle, listening at the door. Inside the board seems to have concluded all their business.

'I must thank all you distinguished board members' says Dennis in a voice rich with smarm. 'And apologise, although nothing to do with me, for the scandalous scenes you have witnessed this morning.' One of the prelate's muses that he's seen a lot more inventive girl-on-girl action at one of the many discreet venues he patronises when he can get away, but this he keeps to himself. The table falls into individual discussions about where they will have lunch, when they will return home, and (the men in business suits) whether or not they will take out a hit on Alec for outraging Christian morals.

Suddenly the door is again flung open, causing Sandra and Rochelle, skulking in the corridor, to scuttle away. In strides a person unknown to most of the board. But not to Dennis.

Jerry has never been one for unpaid public performances. He's not that happy to be giving his all merely to do his former boyfriend, Zac, a favour. However, he's also pissed off that Dennis dumped him without a financial send-off so he's agreed to show himself this morning.

'Yeah' he says in laconic greeting. 'So I'm here because you guys are being sold a bill of crap. I make my living as a sex pig.' That, thinks the more sensitive board members, explains the unusually overripe stench now pervading the room. We thought a dozen athletes in dire need of a shower were lining up to sing us out the building.

'So a sex pig, if you don't know what that means' he says looking at several male members of the board who clearly do, 'is someone who allows a man with a fetish for filth to get his rocks off. And there's one man in this room who fits that description.' A couple of bishops panic momentarily and are then relieved when Jerry points an unclean finger at Dennis.

'Who – how – How did you know to come here?' splutters Dennis.

'That's not exactly the point' replies Philip, 'but if you must know for the sake of completeness, I silently texted Adam what had gone down here. And he texted Jerry who came here in the nick of time. To confront you with your own sordid personal indiscretions.'

'I've never seen this man in my life' cries Dennis, but in such a weak and high voice no one believes him.

Dennis, though, still has a card left to play. He strides to the door and calls to Alec and Sandra, standing abandoned and forlorn in the corridor, still unable to take in what has just happened and reluctant to finally quit the building they have known so many years. At the door Dennis puts an arm around both of them and whispers 'Bygones be bygones. Stick together. Together we're the only ones who know how the company works. They can't fire all three of us.'

Twenty-Three. ALEC & FAMILY

'They can't fire all three of us, huh' sneers Sandra bitterly. Following an upsetting and vicious showdown between the board and the three of them, during which Mother Agnes threw biscuits, they were ignominiously escorted from Bland's. They have now taken refuge in a high street café. She watches as Rochelle, ever the professional, balances cartons of coffee times five as she weaves her way back to their banquette.

'Thanks, PeePee darling.'

'Most welcome, oh Queen.'

While several parched throats gingerly sip their hot drinks Dennis, looking malevolently in Sandra's direction, sees she is munching a Romany Cream. His stomach growls in a famished and jealous way.

'Where'd you get that?' he snaps.

'Found it in my hair' says Sandra mildly.

Dennis looks gloomily around the café.

'Suppose I could always get a barista job here' reckons Dennis.

'I hate you. You stupid man. Why didn't you tell me that's what you had planned?' snaps Sandra.

'How was I to know Philip can be such a fast thinker? He's never impressed me as a PA.'

'Piss off wanker' responds Philip, no longer regarding Dennis as his boss. There is a flurry of activity in the direction of their banquette and Darryl arrives, having calculated, correctly, that someone else will foot the lunch bill. He instantly reads the atmosphere and sits quietly, snapping off acrylic nails in a passive-aggressive manner.

'I'm too upset to think about what I do next' says Alec. 'All I've ever known is Bland's.'

'Are you going to have to sell your lovely home?' asks Darryl, anxiously. Alec dismisses this prospect with a careless shake of his grizzled head. Darryl relaxes.

'It's just such a pity' says Dennis. 'I mean, at this table there is a wealth of commercial talent. We know each other. I'm not denying that Sandra, and to a lesser extent myself, took a wrong turn, let things run out of control, but we're here, we're unexpectedly available, surely we can find a way forward as a group?'

'First' replies Sandra, 'getting rid of Alec was all your bad. I don't deny I helped it along but don't try to rewrite history.'

'All that is irrelevant' whines Dennis, 'listen to the message. We shouldn't give up. From the ashes we can rise with a new company, a new vision.'

'Or I can retire and look after Adam. I have a vision of building a home which Darryl can share' says Alec thoughtfully.

Darryl, who up till this moment has been studying the menu, looks up. 'I like that. I'll go for that' he says, meaning the vision not the menu.

'And it's all very well to say we should stay together' mumbles Alec. 'Exactly what would we do? All I know is religious memorabilia. And Bland's has a stranglehold on the world market.'

This sobering reality has the effect of turning everyone's attention to the menu. They order. The food arrives. Not much happens in between. The group feels too despondent to speak.

'Except' says Darryl, now speaking with spirit, having enjoyed a nourishing meal on someone else's dime, 'we're looking at this thing from the wrong direction. Alec, it's not that you only know religious stuff. It's that you have many years of marketing and commercial experience which up till now has only been applied in that way. I've been looking through all the product you keep at home.' This informal research began as a quest to find something in all the piles that could be sold on. After hours of sifting Darryl reached the disappointing conclusion that you need to be transfixed by religious fervour before any of the merchandise looks inviting.

'How about we think totally laterally. Alec is a great Chair/MD. Dennis could be Operations Manager. Sandra, assisted by Rochelle, could focus on women's needs. And Philip, even though he's not the world's best PA, knows something about the Twink market.'

Alec has not really been following. 'I'm sorry, what is the Twink market?'

'Oh' says Darryl, 'didn't I explain that part? It's just that sitting here it occurred to me that together we cover the whole lesbian and gay market. We'll need to drag Jerry out of some gutter then he can be our expert on the sleaze.'

Dennis raises an immaculately manicured hand, which everyone can't help admiring. 'Sorry, if I'm to understand you right, you want us to be *pornographers?*'

'No, not pornographers, silly' says Darryl with an amused chuckle. 'Gay porn. It's totally different.'

'Sorry,' continues Dennis, in a tone which carries the implication that he's not sorry in the slightest, 'you're suggesting we *expose ourselves*? We stand up and say to the world 'I'm gay and not only am I gay but I'm so gay I spend my days manufacturing, packaging and distributing porn? I'm outraged! I've never heard such a disgusting suggestion in my life!'

'Oh girl,' Darryl responds, 'I can't believe that! You forget I know *exactly* how you've spent your down time.'

Dennis frowns. 'Yes. Perhaps because of the strain, the insane demands put on me, I wanted to experience something in my downtime that was a real break from all the pressure. But I'm ex-public school. We're screwed up but we keep it strictly under the counter. You're suggesting we align ourselves with all that is loathsome and vile in human beings!'

Darryl snaps back. 'No I'm not. I have to tell you I'm not happy with some of that rubbish they call porn. Guys beating other guys and humiliating them. But what's wrong with celebrating our sexuality and racking up sales at the same time?'

'Okay but in that case we're going to have to be careful around kink' says Dennis, his mind still on his recent brush with mortality, even if it did happen to Guy and not him. 'I think I could go an ex-rated version of *How Clean is Your Home?'*

'I think' begins Alec before he's overwhelmed by other voices.

'How dare you assume Rochelle and I are okay with women's porn! It's degrading! It's just another way for men to exploit women.'

'Exactly!' says Darryl. 'So in our company women will make the porn for women. Which also means they'll know what women actually appreciate, rather than what men give them. Remember *50 Shades*? Let's empower all women to celebrate their sexual natures!'

People at other tables are staring at this one. The participants are too involved to notice.

'Actually' starts Alec before he is drowned out.

'Why do we have to go from religion to porn?' asks Dennis. 'Why can't we use our resources for something non-threatening?'

'Because' says Alec, and for some reason everyone stops talking and listens, 'because it would be the surest way of saying to the world, and to ourselves, that we are no longer ashamed. That we see nothing wrong in sex and our sexual preferences. That we wish to completely divorce ourselves from the scared, shrivelled, disabled people we have been up till now. That we are beautiful, strong, and horny.'

Someone a couple of tables away begins to applaud. Our table is still too involved to notice.

'So let me get this right' says Dennis. 'Up till now I've been so guilty about being gay that I've beaten myself up. I've got involved in humiliation and heavy cleaning. I've tried to make up for being gay by working for a company making religious memorabilia. But in this new way of looking at our lives, since we *are* gay, surely it makes the best sense if we go all-out to use our being gay not only for the greater good but also because we need to make a living?'

'That's beautiful' murmurs Rochelle. Up till now she has said nothing. Inside she has been picturing a line of soft pink rubber dental dams, hygienic, practical, romantic, perhaps called 'la Sandra'.

Sandra takes in Rochelle's enthusiasm but has a big fat fly to dump.

'And how, genius, are we going to pay for this operation? It takes millions to start up a company from scratch.'

'Well' says Alec, 'we're not really from scratch. The legwork and heavy lifting's already in place. All we have to do is go round Bland's existing suppliers and explain our new needs. We might have to slip them a few extra pounds to work over the weekend, but I think we can overcome any objections.'

‘Again with the money’ says Sandra. ‘I’ve yet to hear where it’s coming from.’

‘I thought that was obvious’ says Alec, puzzled. ‘You must remember I’m a hugely wealthy man. I spend my leisure hours deciding which organisations I’m going to leave my money to. I’d sooner spend it on this delightful new enterprise.’

‘So we’d be on salary from the beginning?’ asks Dennis swiftly.

‘We’d *all* be on salary?’ asks Darryl, equally fast off the mark.

‘You’ll need a competent PA’ says Philip.

Alec favours Philip with a charming smile.

‘Oh’ says Philip, ‘I’m not thinking of me. I’m totally crap, ask Dennis. I’ve got friends though who would be excellent.’

‘Then what will you do?’ asks Alec. ‘I wouldn’t like us to lose you.’

‘I’ve got other skills’ says Philip. ‘No one at work ever asks what I’ve been doing at the weekend. I write gay romance novels. I’ve got about a dozen already and lots more ideas.’

‘Wonderful’ says Alec. ‘Now all we need is a company brand.’

‘How about DAS – Dennis, Alec, Sandra’ suggests Dennis, naturally.

‘Rubbish name’ says Sandra. How about Sandra – Alec – Dennis?’

‘You want to call us the SAD company?’ snaps Dennis.

‘We’ll call ourselves’ says Alec, pausing for effect, ‘the ABB company.’

‘To exploit how people like ABBA?’ asks Philip.

'ABB stands for Anything But Bland. They won't be able to legally stop us trading because, frankly, we won't be dealing in the same territory.'

There is a brief silence while the table digests the new turn of events and the indifferent meals.

'Does anyone want to read one of my novels?' asks Philip in the silence.

'No thanks' says Dennis. 'No time.'

'Here's my elevator pitch. They're all kind of the same thing. Young guy meets really old guy. Old guy has been looking for love. In the wrong places. So finally, really old guy and young guy get together.'

'That would definitely fit one section of the market' admits Dennis cautiously. 'But are you sure what you write is authentic?'

'Oh definitely' says Philip, looking meaningfully at Alec. 'No one ever asks me about my private life, but I'm a dedicated grandad shagger.'

This announcement somehow draws a line under the discussion. With a lot to think about, yet definitely excited and beginning to plan on how to usher the dream into reality, the group breaks up.

'I've got to get back to Adam' says Darryl.

'I must say, dear man,' says Alec, 'I'm touched. I was a little dubious about you at the beginning, now I see you are genuinely fond of Adam.'

'Why are people always surprised when I act like a human?' asks Darryl. 'I'm really a very nice person.'

'And you're smarter than you look' adds Dennis, thinking this a generous compliment.

'Piss off' responds Darryl.

On the pavement, while Rochelle and Philip flag down taxis, Alec turns to Sandra, Dennis and Darryl.

'I think we should have an away weekend. To put down on paper our next moves. Blythe Hall springs to mind.'

'Do they have women weekends?' asks Sandra.

'I can take over the place for a couple of days' says Alec. 'You really must remember that I'm enormously wealthy.'

'I won't ever forget' promises Darryl. 'I've been thinking of an appropriate signing bonus. I've always wanted a Rolex. Pink gold. With a diamond bezel.'

Before Darryl can think of any more bling to add, Sandra and Rochelle, and Dennis, depart in taxis. Alec, Darryl and Philip climb into another.

On the way home to Hampstead, Philip discreetly puts his hand on Alec's knee. Alec does not remove it.

Twenty-four. ALEC.

The other day I read that Norman Fowler, the only Tory I admire, has started a new AIDS awareness campaign. In the article he notes that 'I'm only 83 and unless I'm careful I won't have time to start my new career.' I like his spunk. For so many years I watched life passed by and all I got was older. Now I think of myself 'I'm only 72…'. And people say the same thing to me. Well, principally Philip.

Sandra and Rochelle got married and they both wore dresses which caused a minor sensation. Dennis decided to pursue Ted, who agreed to go out with him if Dennis took out insurance into the tens of millions. Adam recovered the use of his leg and has seldom been seen standing upright since. He's rekindled his romance with Jerry, who's given up being a professional sex pig and now runs a florist in a very grand location near Covent Garden Opera House. The rest of us, as planned, are the management team behind AAB, your one-stop, nurturing, gay porn suppliers.

Several of the old board at Bland's never recovered from the scandal surrounding my coming out, and the various financial irregularities subsequently uncovered. The police raided not only Bland & Co's offices but also the board's private homes. Funny how they thought an anonymous tip-off was to blame, perhaps I should have done more owning about my discreet talks with the vice squad? Anyway, I thought the archbishop's sentence was quite lenient. Overall the publicity was marvellous for us, so it just goes to show that even the bigoted, hypocritical church can be helpful at times. Mother Agnes, briefly incarcerated before the police agreed to drop her charges on the grounds that she's senile, revived to such an extent that she's been proclaimed a Living Saint.

Philip and I are very happy together. Recently we even explored the possibility of a threesome. His choice of third party, of course. He found some decayed fossil who could still walk up stairs and I organised a special dinner. Cocktails beforehand, champagne, red wine with the three courses. Coffee, chocolates, liqueurs. Quite interesting conversation. Then Philip discreetly excused himself to prepare the bedroom and when he came back to fetch us, me and the third party were sound asleep. Philip was quite annoyed and since then we've been sticking to monogamy.

THE END

Printed in Great Britain
by Amazon